I0618445

Billionaire Unloved

Billionaire Romance Series

J.L. Ryan

Published by J.L. Ryan, 2018.

BILLIONAIRE UNLOVED

First edition. June 2, 2018.

Copyright © 2018 J.L. Ryan.

ISBN: 978-1393678120

Written by J.L. Ryan.

The Billionaire's Desire

Young billionaire, Alexander Jacobs knew his life would be different from now on. Nothing could prepare him for the changes that were soon coming. Had he known, he would have done things differently, prepared somehow. He would have tried to make his father proud of him, he would have loved his mother more.

He hung his head in his hands. There was nothing he could do now. His life was changed, and all he had left to focus on was tomorrow. Everything seemed too quiet now. His parents were both gone. They were killed by a drunk driver, he had no siblings, and only a few friends he could count on, friends he could trust that is.

He sat in the high-backed chair and took a deep breath. Even the friends he did have were busy with their own lives. He was 27 years old and still too young to know what he was doing most of the time. Now, he was going to have to run the family business that he hadn't much thought about before.

He enjoyed the fruits of the family business. He always had everything he needed or wanted. He was spoiled and selfish. He shook his head because he knew that he would have to grow up fast.

Alex glanced up at the clock on the mantle. The meeting started at 2. That gave him ten minutes to get his head together. He started rifling through the ledger on his desk, trying to prepare for the day ahead. His parents had been gone for almost a week. The funeral was yesterday. They deserved more...deserved better. He would do his best to make them proud. He knew he would have to, there was no one else who could.

The only bright spot about yesterday's funeral was that Brienne Warhol was there. He remembered the day he first saw her in 4th grade. She was all elbows and freckles with her long red hair in braids. She was beautiful. They grew up in the same town, but were raised very differently. His family was wealthy, while her parents worried about where the next meal would come from.

She was always a gangly tomboy who loved playing in the dirt and riding bikes with the boys. All the other girls were happy playing inside with their Barbie dolls and practicing putting on make-up and nail polish. He smiled thinking about the 6th grade dance.

He prepared to ask her for weeks. She never seemed to notice he was there because she always busy with something else. Most of the boys thought of her as one of them. Not Alex, he was very much aware of the fact that Brienne was a girl. He had it all planned out and walked up to her at lunchtime. She was sitting at a table with some of their friends who were arm wrestling each other. He took a deep breath and simply said:

"Brienne, will you go to the dance with me?" He said it casually, despite the fact that his heart was racing a mile a minute.

"Sure." She said it so quickly that he had to look at her to catch her eye and make sure she was actually responding to him. She gave him a slight smile and set out to arm wrestle, and beat, Bobby Anderson on the next match.

His dad sent him in a company car to pick her up the night of the dance and he was terrified. She came down the stairs in a green dress and her hair all brushed out, fluffy like orange cotton. She was beautiful. He opened the door for her, and once they were inside she started chattering away about school and how her "girly" shoes were so dumb.

He just let her talk. He liked the way she went on and on. He was always the quiet one and she didn't know how to be. It may have been because she had no mother, and her dad was doing the best he could with her. Whatever the reason, she always had a lot to say. They pulled into the school parking lot and waited for their group of friends to show up. It was just like any other school day. At some point, she braided her hair so it would stop "flying all over the place" as she put it.

The rest of the night was spent having fun with their other classmates. No dancing, and certainly not what he planned.

He smiled as he was brought back to the present. She came to the funeral. She was there for him, and he loved her all the more for it. They were friends now, not as close, but still friendly enough. She would send him emails from school and he would write back talking about whatever was going on in their sleepy town of Dale City Virginia.

He enjoyed the way she would write about her classes and about the men who asked her out. She went off to New York after high school because she dreamed of going to Columbia Law. She thought her best option would be to complete her undergraduate work there as well.

Brienne always worked hard to do well. Alex would frequently ask if she was okay and if she needed anything. She always told him no. She was defiant and determined to succeed. He admired that in her. He went to college locally at Mary Washington and studied Business. He had no clue what he wanted to do, and his father told him it was a great back up for whenever he figured it out.

Today he was thankful for that. Seeing her yesterday after such a long time was amazing. Gone were the braids and freckles, and in their place, was a sophisticated woman. She was still as beautiful as the day he met her. He never even had a chance to speak with her. She gave him a wave at one point and he smiled back.

She was rarely in town, and when she was, he always tried to make time for her. They would usually eat Chinese take-out and laugh, and listen to music from the year they graduated. The last time she visited was over two years ago. Even then, she hadn't strayed much from The Brienne of middle school. It was obvious something changed. Yesterday, he was surrounded by his parents' friends and business associates. By the time he was able to get a few moments alone to visit with Brienne, she disappeared.

It would be easy to find her. She was staying with her father, who lived in the same house where she grew up. Her home was located in a small mill town, while Alex and his family enjoyed living in their gated mansion a couple miles away. His parents planned on having more children, but it never come to pass.

He had every intention of going to see her tonight. After this meeting of course. He stood and grabbed his paperwork, took a deep breath, and headed down the corridor. He could do this.

Two hours later, Alex pulled forcefully on the tie at his throat. What a mess. The merger was two days away when his parents were killed. He wanted to go home and grieve but this paperwork had to be done before something, or someone, showed up to rock the proverbial boat. He spent two hours being briefed about acquisitions and merger paperwork.

The logistics of operations, and the appointing of officers to manage the foreign accounts was almost too much for him to handle. Most of which he was in the dark about, but he would learn, he had too. The only person he trusted was Jameson, who was his father's trusted advisor and best friend. He was the one who prepared him for today and the one who would help him take the business to a new level. He would be okay, he had no choice.

Alex headed home to organize the pieces of his life he could still control, and to change and relax before tackling the next big thing that would inevitably come up. The driver pulled up to the gate and they moved on until they rounded the front of the house. Not really one for the rules, Alex jumped out of the car as they stopped. He refused to wait for the chauffeur to open the door for him, as he was capable and refused to follow all of the rules.

He bounced up the front stairs and opened the door to the main hall. He could smell his mother's perfume when he entered the house. He hoped it would always be that way, but sadly, time erases everything. He made his way upstairs and changed into jeans and a t-shirt. He was sure being seen in town dressed so casually was something frowned upon now that he was the head of the business. He was suddenly forced to become his father. The thought made him cringe as his father had been stern and fair, but not easily approachable. His mother was the nurturer and his father, the businessman.

Alex ran a hand through his black hair and looked at his reflection for a moment. He had lines around his eyes. The stress was already taking a toll, and it had been days.

He dated his fair share of women, enjoyed having fun, and meeting different people. He would figure out his new life as he went along. He shrugged and grabbed his jacket as he headed out. He decided to walk. The April air was crisp and clean, and it helped him to clear his head.

Brienne always had something to say that would make sense, make it better. She never indicated she was interested in Alex at all. Once upon a time he thought she was the one for him, but instead, they only become good friends. That was worth so much more than romance or sex. He walked the quarter mile in silence thinking about his parents. They loved each other very much. They were always together, and the night of the accident was no different.

His father was hosting a dinner party to raise funds for one of his business mergers. His mother accompanied him, ever devoted to her husband. They said goodbye to Alex that night as he watched television in the den eating a snack. He yelled a hello and gave them a wave and a glance before they left. Why didn't he go say goodbye the right way, why hadn't he hugged his mother? The fact that he barely gave them a wave made his resolve that much stronger. He would make his parents proud.

He made his way up the driveway of the house Brienne grew up in. It was small and quaint, but clean. Even now, her ten-speed bike was propped up against the side of the house. Untouched in years, it was a symbol of a childhood long gone. She opened the door before he even knocked.

"Alex." She smiled at him, opened the screen door, and came out on the porch. She hugged him tightly. "I'm so sorry about your parents."

She stood back, and he took her in. She was more beautiful than he could remember. She finally tamed her hair and was dressed in a black dress. She was elegant, and he was lost.

"My dad is getting his treatments so I thought I should come outside to you." She walked over to the swing on the porch. Her father was sick, he thought. She had such a hard life growing up but she was strong. They sat on the swing together for a few moments and chatted about the weather. She asked about work and he shared and she told him about school and how soon after she graduated she would be going to Columbia. She had been accepted.

"Hey brat you made it in?" He sat up quickly.

"Yes, I did." She nearly sparkled with the excitement.

"Wow that's great Brie that is wonderful. You worked so hard, I know you're excited." He grabbed her hand and gave her a squeeze.

"Thanks, I am overwhelmed really. I have so much to do to get ready and...well there is a lot." She smiled at him.

"Well we have to go to dinner tonight and celebrate, my treat." He offered and she accepted.

"We never get to hang out anymore, like old times." She sighed. "It was so much easier when we were kids. No one was sick and we all had each other. We had our family we had friends." She sighed.

"It certainly has changed, you're still a brat though." He looked at the tree across the street, thinking. He stood up to go. "I'll pick you up at 6, surprise restaurant, and wear something nice." He smiled at her as she stuck her tongue out at him. He made his way back up the hill towards the bend in the road which would lead back to his house.

Damn you, Alex. She watched him leave. He was so handsome, that was all she could think about. He had always been so damn handsome. It made it hard for her to concentrate when he looked at her. She hated the way he called her brat. He'd done it since they were in middle school. She looked down at the slippers she was wearing. They were so different, she and Alex. Once upon a time she thought he had a crush on her. It was probably at that horrible dance in 6th grade when she figured out he just wanted to be friends. He picked her up and she tried so hard to look pretty.

Her father enlisted help from the neighbor to help with "girl stuff." They did their best. No one knew about conditioner yet and she'd had hair the size of a beach ball. He picked her up and they went to the dance. She talked him to death. It's what she did when she was nervous.

Everyone thought she was just one of the guys and in some ways, she was. She loved playing football and wrestling and she hated getting dressed up. But there was something about Alex that made her feel funny. Looking back she knew it was because he made her feel like a girl. Feeling like a girl was a new idea for her that was for sure. Once they arrived at the dance mean Mary Jenkins pulled her aside in the bathroom and told her about the "bet".

The boys all bet that she would be "different" if she dressed like a girl. She knew then they were testing her, fearful their friendship would be gone for good. So she braided her hair in the bathroom, and went back to being one of the guys. She refused to allow her heart to hurt because she wanted Alex to like her. They were all friends and that was more important than anything else and they didn't want to lose her.

Even now she shook her head as she thought about it. The entire "group" was disbanded by now. Two of the group members left for the military. One was a teacher in town, one was killed in a boating accident, one was a police officer two towns over, and then there was she and Alex. It was funny that they were the only two who didn't have people in their lives. That alone made no sense. Alex was not only the most eligible bachelor in Dale City he was gorgeous to boot. It made no sense at all.

She picked the pillow cushion on the seat as she swung lightly. She was no angel. She dated her fair share of men. Most of them where playboys and only wanting one thing from her. As she took her education more seriously, they took her less seriously. What she wanted was an equal, but who knew if that even existed. Alex was always out of her league anyway, he was rich, refined and charming, and she was all tomboy and barely had enough money to get through school.

Even today he in his designer jeans and she in her slippers with a hole in the big toe. She laughed lightly. They were on opposite ends of reality but they were friends and that was enough for her. She sighed, time to check on her father.

She made her way through the house and cringed. It was a mess. She hated leaving him alone for so long. She hadn't been home in two years. It was just too expensive to come home, she needed every penny for school. He said he understood but it was hard for him. He had gotten sick some time ago and it never seemed to go away. He had breathing treatments and on the phone he always told her he was fine, being here now she knew he had been lying. The house was turned upside down. TV dinners and coffee seemed to be a staple for him and he had no one to come check on him. She found a clean spot on the couch in the living room and sat down to start planning her course of action and what she would tackle first.

A few hours later she looked around her. It was better than she had expected. She scrubbed every inch of the living room and kitchen. There wasn't a speck of dirt on anything and the four large trash bags on the front porch was a testament to her hard work. She was filthy. Her hair in braids and wearing jeans and a tank top, she was a visible mess. Her father spent the afternoon resting and it wasn't until there was a knock on the front door that she even considered how long she had been at it. She opened the front door to find Alex standing there. He was perfect. Blue suit and tie white shirt. His hair brushed back, he could have been on the cover of a magazine. She stood there for a moment before the realization set in that she had been working much longer than she realized. He smiled at her and it brought her back to reality quickly.

"Alex, I ...well see the thing is." She looked down at herself and he cut her off.

"I'm early brat, you have time to get ready unless you want to change the plan and do something more industrial?" She threw a rag at him and he chuckled. The truth was she was adorable. Hair in braids and cleaning, it was like he stepped back in time for a moment. He needed that moment. He felt normal even if for only a few moments. He settled onto a bar stool and watched her head upstairs to get ready.

"I'll hurry Alex, I promise." She called down the stairs to him.

"Just wash your hair, whatever you do, I think I saw a candy bar wrapper in there." He smiled.

"Ha ha very funny mister fancy pants."

He heard the bathroom door shut and the water come on. She always kept him amused if nothing else. He looked around the house. Her father was alone here and it was cozy. He much preferred a smaller space when being alone. It was nice - almost like the house was hugging you. Unlike the space Alex had at home. He was alone in a tremendous amount of space. She bounded down the stairs and the transformation was astounding. She straightened her hair somehow and was wearing a dark blue dress with a square cut neckline and black pumps. Her face was alive with pink cheeks and some light gloss on her lips. Otherwise she was without make up.

"You gonna stare at me like I have two heads or are we going, Mr. Jacobs?" She put her hands on her hips and tapped her foot. He shook himself free of his thoughts and stood so they could go. The drive was pleasant and uneventful. He decided to drive them himself and made reservations in the town nearby.

They had reservation for 7 and he knew she was always multitasking so his early arrival was on purpose. They dined on oysters and salads, and he ordered steak for his main course and she the fish. They chatted about the past and who was where. It was over dessert when a burly looking man came over to say hello.

"Alex and Brie...now if Junior and Jerry were here I'd be rich right now." He smiled and Alex stood and embraced his friend. Brie did the same and kissed Brandon on the cheek. He was part of the "group" and had managed to stay close by. He wasn't in uniform but Alex knew he become a cop a year or so ago. He was always the jokester of the group which made his profession that most interesting. He had always been the one to get them into trouble and now he was the one enforcing the rules.

"Just look at you two, how long has it been two three years?" Alex motioned for him to sit and he did so.

"My buddies and I are out celebrating a big bust we took down earlier today. I have to get back but after seeing "Red," over here." He hooked his thumb towards Brie. "I just had to come say hello."

Brie smiled at him. "You look great and congrats on the bust."

"I look the same, you on the other hand look great." He leaned towards her obviously flirting and joking at the same time.

"Sorry to hear about your folks Alex man, really. I was at the funeral but you were surrounded by people." He sobered for a moment.

"Thanks Bran that means a lot to me." Alex took a long drink. "So why would you be rich?"

"Oh yea that." He chuckled "A long time ago Jerry and Junior and I made a bet on who was going to marry Brie. They said Mason but not me, I said Alex. We all put two bucks in and buried it under the old cotton mill steps." He laughed and they joined in.

"Well we're not married so you'd still not be rich, besides that money was spent a long time ago." Alex smiled at the shocked look on his face.

"Well you two look married enough all fancy and laughing I just assumed..." he trailed off as Brie took a long drink of water. "Wait what do you mean that money was spent a long time ago?"

"Well the thing is Mason and I heard about your bet and we dug that money up and bought soda pop and chips one afternoon. We sat by the old mill and laughed at how we pulled one over on you all." Alex laughed at the look on his face.

"Well damn, and here I thought I had $6 in savings I could count on." He smiled at them and stood up. "I have to get going, y'all look real nice together so don't fight the love people." He sauntered off giving Brie a wink as he went.

"Well Bran has certainly not changed a bit." Brie changed the subject as to avoid and discussion about love.

"Have I told you that you look beautiful tonight Brie? I'm slow so I doubt I have but I wanted you to know it."

He gave her a half smile and she blushed. What was wrong with him anyway, he was being awfully flirty. They wrapped up dinner and he headed back to her house. She had always been easy to talk to and having this time together was wonderful. She helped him feel more like himself than he had in a long time. They sat on the porch swing for a while. He wanted to enjoy laughing for a little while longer.

"When do you head back?" He glanced over at her on the swing.

"Tomorrow." She looked down at her hands. "I have registration Monday and classes start next week. I feel like I should turn it all down though. Dad, he is just not well and I worry about him."

"You can't turn it down Brie, you have to go. I can check in on him from time to time. You have worked too hard to quit now."

She looked over at him. "Really, you'll check on him? That's an awful lot to ask of you Alex, you have a company to run." She leaned back.

"Yes really, it will bring me back to reality from time to time." He smiled. He stood up from the swing. He knew if he stayed too long he'd make a fool of himself like he did long ago. She didn't think of him like "that" and he didn't want her to feel uncomfortable. He especially didn't want to ruin their friendship.

He gave her a hug and she leaned into it. If only he didn't think of her like a boy. She knew he didn't want to ruin their friendship, but it was hard not to want him to see who she was now. He was her best friend and that would have to be enough.

"I'll be back in June maybe we can do this again?" She smiled at him.

"Of course, you know that." He was being polite in his words when what he wanted to do was kiss her.

They parted ways both thinking of the other. The night was long for them both. What they didn't realize is that life was about to change and it would be much longer than just June before they would see each other again.

Days turned into weeks and then months. Soon it had been a year since his parents had died. Alex was learning his new role proficiently. He had a hand in the last two accounts and things were looking up. He tried to do well, tried to think like his father and it had paid off. He would get an email from Brie from time to time about classes and work but time between them grew wider and wider, she worked all the time it seemed. He checked in on Mr. Warhol every Sunday and he was doing remarkably well. He even had a lady friend that came around. He would leave voicemails for Brie occasionally and tell her about her father, but never heard back.

The months grew longer and the contact slowly grew more sporadic. He was busy with work and it consumed him. He dated a cute blonde from legal for a while a few months ago, but the drive to do better created some distance between the two of them. He was alone. Once the solitude had frightened him but now he felt solace in numbers and accounting. One day he was reading the papers when he saw an article about a drug bust in Manassas. There on the page was Bran's ugly mug smiling happily like he hadn't a care in the world. He was promoted and Alex smiled. He deserved it. He read the article and was even more surprised that he was getting married as well.

"Well, well, well, Brandon. I can't believe you're taking the plunge." Alex grinned thinking about when he saw him last at the restaurant. He and Brie were having dinner. What was that a year ago now? He shook his head time was flowing by so fast. Brie...he hadn't thought about her in a while. He hoped she was doing well at school. Her curriculum was difficult, that much he knew. He decided to send her a quick email. He hadn't heard from her in 3 or 4 months now.

"Just checking in to say hello, hope your well. Your dad looks great and is happy with his new lady friend. Keep in touch.

A

He signed it with his initial as always. He went back to the proposition on his desk, there was always work to be done and this particular company had a lot of excess baggage that would have to be trimmed. He worked through lunch and finally raised his head after the sun went down. Dinner was a rush of snacks and coffee. He rarely had time for anything else.

"Alex, you need to take better care of yourself." Jameson had come into the office and was sitting on the edge of the couch.

"I know Jameson...so you tell me every other day." He said it quietly but with a smile on his face.

"I mean it Alex you need to get out and live, meet a nice girl ..." he trailed off.

"There is no time for all of that, Jameson and you well know it. So much time was lost in the early days when I was learning and now I have to make it right. When I do, I'll go out and have fun as you put it."

Jameson gave a huff as he stood to go. "Lady Alice is here to see you Alex perhaps she can keep you...ah...company for a while." He left and Alex scowled slightly as she came in. She was petite and blonde and liked to be serious. It may have been her education but she rarely laughed as it would make people think she was "a silly blonde" and not take her seriously.

"Hello Alex." She held up her had to stop him from saying anything. "I know we haven't seen each other in a while, but I was hoping we could go over a case I'm working on and at least share a meal. It's a lonely business and I don't have many people I trust. Besides you make me feel smart and pretty, I like that combination and quite frankly, I need some stress relief." She smiled at him.

He was never been one for settling down but she was right. It was a lonely existence when you're in this world. She was smart and she was pretty. He could use the distraction. Besides, she presented it as if their relationship could be some kind of business arrangement and, much like her career she was very determined to do things perfectly, their sex life had been no different. He smiled at her.

"Agreed Alice, agreed. I would love to work on it with you, I just can't give you more than you're asking for right this moment." He looked at her directly. He wanted to be honest up front.

"Once I thought I wanted marriage and family Alex, but I can see clearly now that work is a better path for me. I'm happy with friends, with some benefits. I'd rather have someone in my bed I trust than someone I love." She took off her gloves and settled into the sofa as Jameson came back in.

"Dinner?" He glanced towards Alex.

"Yes Jameson, can you order food for us and have one of the drivers pick it up. Miss Alice and I have some work we need to do." He never looked away from Alice, and Jameson smiled. At least this was a start. Time went on for a while and the mutual benefits to the relationship kept both Alex and Alice happy. She was thriving at work and was looking for new work in a bigger firm. Alex couldn't have been happier at work. Things were thriving and he was content. Each night he went to bed alone which was when he would over think things and what he wanted. He was happy, he had money, and he had a beautiful lover. What was missing? He would go to bed each night wondering why he couldn't just be content. Even Mr. Warhol married his lady friend. Was there more out there?

Brienne was in very much the same position. She worked and worked and never had a moment's peace. The tuition depleted her savings and there was no hope for paying for her final two years unless she worked. She was working in the law library in the mornings, she had classes in the afternoon and evening, and was working in a bar after class at night.

Days seemed to fly by and with her strange hours, time was a relative thing. She needed to go see her father...or at least call him. He met someone and had a quick wedding. She was happy for him, after so long he deserved to be happy. Plus, she knew he was being taken care of. She received an email from Alex a few months ago.

She hadn't even found time to reply to that. She heard he was dating Alice Pope, it was a name that popped up in news articles she read about him. His business was doing well, extremely well from what she understood. She didn't want to bother him with stupid emails from an old friend. He was nice enough to send her a hello and for that she was thankful. She received an invitation to Brandon's wedding but she knew she couldn't make it.

If she missed one day it would only set her back even more. She met a nice guy at work but she had no time to date. His name was Blake and he would often come sit at the bar with her and walk her to her car. They made small talk and he was nice enough. She knew he wanted more but was concerned about things progressing in a direction that was ultimately going to go badly. Tonight was no exception. He was sitting across the bar laughing with some guy about how the Cowboys were going to beat the Redskins on Monday night. He caught her eye and gave her a wink. He never missed a beat of the conversation and defended his

"Cowboy" honor to a fault. He really was nice. That night after the bar closed, he walked her out and this time he seemed different. He hugged her goodbye and when she turned to go, he pulled her in close for a kiss. She let it go on for a moment, it had been a long time since anyone kissed her. Before she knew it, one thing led to another and she found herself waking up the next day with him in her bed. She stood there now, towel wrapped around her watching him sleeping. It was a fun night, but the connection she was looking for wasn't there. She actually felt bad for letting things get out of hand.

She tiptoed into the shower to get ready for the day, not wanting to wake him up and face where things stood now. She ate a quick breakfast, left a note for Blake and headed downtown to Kirby and Bates where she was working. They were prepping for a huge case and it was all hands on deck for sure. She sat in the conference room combing through files and let her mind drift for a second. She felt different somehow, yes she had a fun night but it was something else. Perhaps she just felt old. She smiled.

Alex would tell her she wasn't old, she just lived like it. Alex, he was so different from anyone else. Blake was not Alex....why she even thought it was bothersome enough. She spun around and got back to work. This stack of paperwork would not sort itself, that much was sure. She worked through her day excited about the fact that tomorrow was Saturday.

The law firm was closed and she had no classes so she had the day free until work tomorrow night. This was her day to run all of her errands and get all of her work done. She could also sleep in past 6:30 am. Her only indulgence was ice cream. Every Saturday afternoon she would get comfortable and eat ice cream and watch an old movie. Only one, she had to study and time was precious.

The day dragged on and after her classes she headed home for a quick bite and to get ready for work. At some point Blake left, and even the bed was made. She changed into her other clothes and headed out. Fridays were always crazy, there were people drinking and laughing, and most of the time there was a fight or two over some woman.

Blake wasn't there, which was odd, but he probably had things to do. Finally, as time went on, Brienne found herself looking at the clock more and more. One more hour, and she had almost a free day to herself. She wrapped things up and headed home. She was exhausted.

She was lucky only one year to go and she could take the bar exam and be done. She was 26 and still young enough where she could build a career and eventually be able to relax. She didn't want to be poor and struggle like she had done all of her childhood.

Her father did his best, but it was easier and cheaper to let her just dress and behave like a boy. She was fine with it, as it gave her friends. Besides, she had no idea what she was "supposed" to act like. Her father was her only role model. He worked long hours and she had to fend for herself a lot of the time. They scraped by enough to keep the house, but food was rare. She went to bed hungry on more than one occasion and she decided she would never do that again. Her career was her foundation and it would make it so that she never went hungry again. She pulled into her lot and made her way to her apartment. It was a small efficiency on the campus. She did tutoring part time three times a week to allow herself the luxury of living alone.

She considered calling Blake but let the idea go. It was fun, but she didn't have time for all of the drama that comes with having a man in her life. Saturday came bright and sunny. She rolled over at it was 8:10. Even that simple thing...sleeping in made her happy. She started her day doing some shopping and settled in at noon for movie time. She frowned because nothing good was on television.

She sighed and turned it off all together and pulled her laptop into her lap. Maybe she could respond to some emails and some articles for her class. Not fun, but it was better than watching TV.

She opened her new emails. She really needed a system. She spent the next two hours replying and writing to professors and classmates, and her father until she finally cleaned the entire thing out. The next email in the list was the one from Alex now 6 months old. Should she? She shrugged.

A,

Life is busy, I hear business is doing well, I saw your article in the Times. She is pretty. I hope you're happy.

Yours,

B

She sat back and ate her ice cream, then gave her father a call to listen to all that was happening back home.

Life went on and on. Alex was now in charge of a corporation ranking number three on the stock exchange. He was secure and enjoying life as much as he could. Tomorrow his parents would have been gone three years. Three years ago he sat in the very chair he was in now. He ran his hand over the cool leather. He not only carried on the business, he also become everything his father wanted him to be and he did it by working hard. Alice moved on and found a position with a firm in Washington. He was alone again. He let his mind drift to thoughts of Brie. She wrote him back and told him Alice was pretty. Why would she say that? Why did he focus on that? He shook his head. Nothing made sense as far as Brienne Warhol was concerned. She found a new life, one that didn't include him. He hadn't seen her in years and only heard from her from time to time.

He sorted through the stack of mail on his desk. He wasn't as overwhelmed now. Experience taught him to know the size of the correspondence and what was probably inside. He found a green postcard and pulled it from the stack. It was an invitation to a graduation. Probably some staff member or associate. He turned it over and felt his heart race a little faster. It was for Brienne. She did it. She was graduating from Columbia and with honors, no less. He leaned back in his chair and smiled. She hadn't completely forgotten him, he thought to himself. May 15th. He had a little less than two weeks. He called Linda the secretary.

"Yes, Mr. Jacobs?"

"Linda clear my schedule for the weekend of May 14th. I'll be out of town for a few days."

"Yes, Mr. Jacobs. I'll take care of it."

"Thanks Linda, and plan the weekend off for you too, paid of course, you deserve it."

"Thank You, Mr. Jacobs!"

He hung up, thinking about the weekend he would be gone. He hadn't been this excited about something in a long time. He decided to stroll down to Mr. Warhol's and see what his plan was for graduation. He remembered the way he felt when he came down here to check on him. He always felt like he was helping Brie somehow. She was far enough away to make it hard to see her father and she never had time to come home anymore. Now he was doing well and he felt like he wasn't needed anymore. He knocked on the door lightly and was greeted by a plump older woman who wore a huge smile.

"Alex, come on in...it's been so long. How have you been?" She enveloped him in a warm hug and shut the door behind him.

He blushed slightly. There was something overwhelmingly motherly about her. She was nothing like his mother in looks or stature but she carried the same warm love about her. Mr. Warhol walked into the room and smiled at Alex.

"Alex, we were just talking about you. Brienne called me a couple of weeks ago and asked about graduation and asked about you." He gave Alex a knowing look.

He swallowed hard. She asked about him? "How is she? I never hear from her, but I just assumed she had a lot of classes this final year."

"She is better than good, she is happy to quit one of her jobs and be able to focus on the bar exam for a while. After graduation I think I have her talked into coming home for a few months until she takes the exam. She needs the break because she works so hard." He sighed.

"What has she been doing exactly? I know she had a full course load and was tutoring, but that's all she really told me." He smiled up as Mrs. Warhol handed him a glass of iced tea.

"She never told you about...work?" Mr. Warhol cleared his throat. "I think maybe she was embarrassed about it or just too busy. I wish

I was able to help her more. She deserved more from me." He turned somber.

"Mr. Warhol, do you remember when all the neighborhood kids would be playing softball in the field and how we broke Old Mr. Sampson's window?" He smiled remembering.

"Oh yes he was fit to be tied, ole Sampson." Mr. Warhol smiled.

"Do you remember when prom came and the car broke down and we were all stuck over the state line trying to buy beer?" Mr. Warhol busted into a fit of laughter at that one.

"You boys would have been in so much trouble." He grinned at Alex.

"Who saved us? Who paid for ole Sampson's window, who came and got us all and helped fix that car and get it home?" He looked at Mr. Warhol. "That is two of many examples I can give you, but you saved us all. We never even thought to go to any other parent because you were the "cool" parent. We are all thankful for you so don't ever think you didn't give us all something." He smiled over at Mr. Warhol who looked about to cry.

"Thanks for that son, I loved every one of you. You protected Brie, kept her from getting into too much trouble. I'm proud of all of you. Your father would be proud of who you've become. With Brie, I just worry. She's still a girl, she works three jobs, and always keeps a good face on, but I'm not sure how hard it's really been on her." He sighed.

"Well you can see when you go to graduation, and at least get an idea of what has been going on. Why is she working three jobs? I ask her every time I talk to her or hear from her if she needs anything. Of course, I never hear from her." He raked his hand in his hair.

"Well she is stubborn our Brie." Mr. Warhol smiled at him. "You probably know that better than anyone else. As for graduation, I'm not sure about all of that just yet." He glances at his wife. "We will have to see."

"You are going aren't you?" Alex sat up. "She needs you there, it's important to her."

"We are going to try that's for certain." Mr. Warhol patted his hand and stood up to refill his drink.

Alex sat back lost in thought. He smiled at Mrs. Warhol who handed him some chocolate cake. He loved the way it felt here. The house that hugs you. He smiled and they went on talking about Brandon's new baby.

The next week and a half, Alex made all of the necessary preparations for the trip. Some of those preparations included securing seats to fly to New York for not only him, but Mr. Warhol and his wife. Money was the issue, though Mr. Warhol didn't want to discuss it.

Alex didn't want to give him any reason to refuse his help. He had the tickets delivered to the house and when Mr. Warhol called to complain, he said they were free with his frequent flyer miles and they were also nonrefundable. He wouldn't want to waste them would he? He didn't think Mr. Warhol bought it, but he relented and was grateful.

They were all leaving in the morning and Alex had some work to complete before he could just leave town. He worked into the night with a sense of excitement. What was wrong with him. It was a graduation not a wedding? He smiled to himself. She was going to be surprised when she saw the three of them show up. They decided to surprise her. He knew she hated surprises, but it serves her right for never writing him back, he thought. He smiled and fell asleep.

The flight was on time and Alex could only grin as he heard Mr. Warhol fuss about first class and how it just "wasn't right." Mrs. Warhol, on the other hand was in awe, and was happily sampling all the food on the flight, much to Alex's' amusement. They settled in for the flight and he drifted off.

Nothing was going right! Brienne was furious. She was pacing for more than an hour waiting to get her final grade in one of her classes. This grade would determine her GPA and ultimately be a huge factor

on her resume. Not only that, she had graduation today and she wasn't
even sure if her father was coming at all. She called him all morning
and nothing. Nothing! She glanced at the clock and hit refresh on the
computer. There it was...A.

She did it. She completed law school at the top of her class. She
was Valedictorian. She swallowed and sat down. She felt the stress of
the last three years melt away. It was worth it. She stood and started
to dance. No one could see her. She was in her own place, so why not.
She bounced around some mix of the hula and the running man. She
stopped in a huff and plopped into the chair.

Today was the day. The day she could start to relax. Her father
asked her to come home for a while....Alex was there. She pushed him
out of her mind. He was probably married to Alice by now. She stood
and gathered her things to head to the graduation. She arrived at the
stadium and was greeted by Professor Abrams who handed her the
tassels to wear for the ceremony.

"Thank You." It's all she could get out. She hoped and prayed for
this moment. She prepared a speech just in case. She knew the running
was between her and one other person. The ceremony began. The usual
lengthy pomp and circumstance, and she made a point of keeping her
speech short and sweet. She focused on the importance of family and
friends, and shared a story from her childhood. She felt the sweet relief
of months of work as she walked across the stage and was handed her
diploma. That's when she saw him.

As she walked down the aisle back to her seat, she saw his blue eyes
and black hair. He was clapping for her as she walked by. He made eye
contact and she felt her knees go weak. What was he doing here? She
could think of nothing else as she waited for the ceremony to end. As
people began to filter out, she was able to find him easily enough. He
towered over most people. He had to be 6 ft. tall. His hair was still dark
and slightly wavy on top now. He looked older and wiser somehow. She
wasn't the only one to be taken back.

Alex stood rooted to the spot. She literally took his breath away. Gorgeous, her red flaming hair was artfully arranged around her shoulders, framing her face. She was wearing heels and a short black dress. She was older, more mature and ...perfect. He swallowed hard as she made her way over to him. She looked to his right and saw her father and his new wife.

"Daddy?" She ran to him and he engulfed her in a hug. It was obvious he was crying.

"I am so proud of you baby girl, you did it!!" He smiled widely and introduced her to his wife. They made small talk for a moment longer when Mr. Warhol cleared his throat and took his wife by the elbow.

"Dear let's make our way to the car, I believe we are going to dinner, Alex, we will meet you at the car." He gave Alex a wink and headed out.

"Hello brat." He smiled at her.

"You know I hate that Alex." She smiled at him anyway. "What are you doing here and how in the world did you find them?"

"I made them come with me on the plane, I don't like being alone. Your father doesn't take help lightly."

"No, he doesn't. I tried to make some extra money to send, but he wouldn't hear of it. You can tell me how much Alex, and I'll get it back to you."

"Don't be ridiculous Brie, think of it as a graduation gift. I brought them here and I'll take them home. Almost like a role reversal from our younger years. I owe him that much. He got me out of so much trouble."

"Like Ole Sampson's window?" she glanced over at him and giggled.

"Exactly." He held the door for her leading outside to the car. He rented a car and driver and she was surprised by the limo that waited for them.

"Alex really?" she looked over at him.

"Happy graduation brat, even if you don't ever call me." He ushered her into the waiting car and they headed to dinner.

It was a happy occasion, everyone was chattering away about everything from graduation to life in Dale City. Brie told them about work and all of the cases she worked on. Eventually, Mr. Warhol announced that he was old and wanted to go back to the hotel. Not one to be disrespectful, Alex asked for the check, which he paid for, despite the protests of the dinner party.

They made their way back to the hotel where Mr. and Mrs. Warhol said their goodbyes and made their way upstairs. Brienne looked at Alex. She was a little tipsy from the champagne at dinner but not so much that she wasn't aware of her surroundings.

"Want to go watch a movie in my room or something?" He asked it casually as though they were still in school, bored on a Friday night.

"Sure, I don't have to go to work tonight." She giggled and Alex looked at her for a long moment. She was working in a bar of all places. She could have been hurt.

They made their way up to his room which had its own living room and she draped herself on the couch unceremoniously. He moved to make some coffee, watching her frustration with her dress being too tight to sit comfortably.

"Hey brat if you want, I have pajamas with me, you could wear them if you want to lose that dress." He froze the moment he said the words. "You know what I mean...they are on the sink in the bathroom."

Brienne made her way into the bathroom and changed. When she returned. She found him artfully arranging cups on a tray. She loved him her whole life and he never even knew she was there. She graduated today and wanted to do something crazy. She walked over to him. He was still in his suit but had lost the tie. She stood as close to him as she could and he braced himself and looked down at her.

She was too close. Something about her made all of the air in the room disappear. She had that mischievous look in her eye he knew so well. What was she up to? He turned to face her and try to figure it out but before he could ask, she threw her arms around him and pulled him down to her. She tasted like honey and champagne. He kissed her back, deeper longer. He pulled her closer to him and put his hands in her hair pulling her closer still.

She didn't know what she was feeling. He was kissing her back and her head was spinning. He was nipping at her mouth when the kiss finally broke. He looked at her with a sad look on his face.

What had she done? He was disappointed. She had crossed a line and would probably ruin their friendship. He just stood there looking at her.

"Alex, I'm so sorry. I just got carried away." She tried to sound reasonable.

"I understand Brie, you just had one too many drinks is all." He turned around to go back to making coffee. He dismissed her entirely. She had hoped...hoped for what? He would suddenly think of her as a girl and not one of his friends? She was a fool. She had to get out of here. She started for the door.

"Brie where are you going?" He saw her at the door. She wouldn't look at him.

"I can't stay Alex not now, I don't know if you can work through this or not but...I just don't know anything." She left the room and headed downstairs. Alex let her go. He called the driver and told him to take her wherever she wanted to go. What was he supposed to do? She never thought of him as anything other than a friend. Now he felt his heart all twisted up just like it had been 15 years ago. Why did she kiss him? Why now? He took a long drink of the coffee.

He sat down in the chair. Was it a game? It made no sense at all. The only thing he could do was try and figure it out.

An hour later he was still plagued with the reaction she caused in him. He buried that a long time ago and one kiss and she drags all of it back out again. It wasn't fair. He stood and grabbed his jacket and called his driver. He needed answers.

Her apartment was on the other side of town. He stood in front of her door and knocked. When she opened the door, he could only stare at her. Still in his pajamas, she braided her hair and washed her face. She looked just like she did years ago, all braids and freckles. She blinked and he shook his head.

"Listen brat I'm not 13 anymore. I don't know what's going on with you but we need to figure it out because I'm all twisted up all over again. He frowned because this was not what he planned to say.

"Thirteen, Alex? What are you talking about? At that age, I was following you around and you didn't even know I existed." She crossed her arms and continued. "I knew all about the bet at the dance and how you all planned to keep me from becoming a girl and all that, Mary Jenkins told me. Its ok I understand. I've had the crush so long I just got overly excited and kissed you, that's all."

He stood there. Bet? What the hell was she talking about and she had a crush?

"First of all there was no bet, Mary Jenkins liked me and told you that to keep us apart. I was half in love with you already then and you just went into tomboy mode as soon as we got there."

He sat down on her couch and she followed. They both sat and thought about it for a while.

"You loved me then?" she whispered it.

"I have always loved you brat." He looked at her.

"I've loved you too Alex, I just wanted you to be happy and you deserved something, someone better." She shrugged.

"There is no one better Brie, this whole time I thought you just saw me as your friend, and I had no idea." He put his hand over hers.

"I thought the same thing Alex." She looked up at him and he smiled before leaning in for another kiss.

This time is was longer deeper and meant more, it held a promise of a future where they could both be less lonely and find happiness and peace. When they separated, Alex began to chuckle.

"What's so funny, mister?" She frowned.

"I think we owe Brandon 6 bucks." They both started laughing and he pulled her into his arms again, this time for good.

******

Unexpected Romance

The blaring alarm clock on the nightstand jolted Jennifer awake. Too groggy to function after a late night at the lab looking over patient case files, she clumsily banged her hand around until she found the annoying culprit and slammed her palm onto the snooze button. Even after years of being lectured that it was better to get up the first time the thing went off, she never could. Only after two snoozes would she allow her eyes to crack open. Not a good habit for a doctor. There were patients to see and research to perform. Who was she kidding? After banging snooze buttons for twenty years, this was one habit she would never break.

After eighteen more luxurious minutes in her cozy warm bed, Jennifer couldn't deny the fact anymore. She had to get up and get going. Waiting any longer and she wouldn't have time for her morning run. No morning run meant a cranky woman—a cranky doctor at that. Not that she enjoyed running but it was the only time she could clear her head completely in order to focus throughout the rest of the day. Caffeine could only help so much so running had become her go-to activity. As much as Jennifer despised the bitter cold of a February morning in the nation's capital, she threw back the covers to begin her day.

It would take at least a mile before the fog of exhaustion began to lift from her mind. The first mile was always the most torturous. After that though, Jennifer could run forever. Adrenaline finally pumping through her petite, 5' 2" frame, she could take on the world. This morning in particular she needed the respite.

Being a pediatric oncologist was her life's dream. That is, after Hannah, her best friend from elementary school suffered horribly and died from a brain tumor. It was the reason she became a doctor in the first place. No child should have to suffer like that, ever. And no parent should have to endure such a loss. But cancer was indiscriminate and unforgiving. Last night she suffered yet another battle with her childhood demon. A three year old child with lymphoma. Jennifer had been so sure her latest protocol would work. She had spent the rest of the night beating herself up for failing yet another patient, another distraught family. Sometimes her life's dream was actually her life's nightmare. This morning she welcomed the punishment of the frigid air filling her lungs as she near sprinted the remaining blocks from her small condominium on K Street to the National Mall. Her destination – the reflecting pond overlooking the Lincoln Memorial.

Once she reached the ice-speckled pond, she allowed herself a moment to rest and take in the beauty of the landscape. Still too early for the onslaught of commuters and tourists who flood the city daily. All was quiet except the occasional rumble of jets overhead as they were taking off from Reagan National. Whether from the freezing temperatures and wind assailing her eyes or from sorrow and frustration at her failure last night, tears ran down her freckled face. Jennifer didn't know what was worse. Losing the patient or the fact that after so many years she still had not toughened up enough to make that pain any less.

Not wishing to dwell on the matter anymore, Jennifer raced back home. Shutting out all thoughts and allowing her body to operate on autopilot. New day, new challenge! She wouldn't allow self-pity to stop her. After many battles lost, and a few won, her determination was greater than ever.

After a quick, scalding hot shower Jennifer towel-dried her short strawberry-blonde locks and made a beeline for the coffee pot. No breakfast. She couldn't remember the last time she actually ate breakfast. Probably before leaving home for college when her overbearing mom would force her to eat before she could leave for school, even if it meant she was late. Her shift didn't start until 10 AM so there was plenty of time to either tidy up her small, 640 square foot condo or aimlessly peruse the internet. Without a second thought, she plopped down in her oversized khaki arm chair with her laptop.

Not obsessed about politics and news like everyone else in this town, Jennifer decided on lighter fare. How long had it been since she'd been on Facebook? Probably since her high school reunion that had been organized via the website, forcing her to get an account. Surprised that she actually remembered her password, the site loaded. Wow! Fifty-two "Friend" requests?! Jennifer was surprised she knew that many people. The newsfeed was filled with funny pictures of cats and babies. Quickly scanning through all the miscellaneous vanities, she noticed a posting from one of her best friends from her days at the University of Colorado. It was a picture of her tall, slender, runway model friend Jacy Standish with her college beau Ethan Davis III. The posting showed the couple with Ethan on one knee and Jacy with the biggest smile ever. Yes, it was the couple's engagement announcement. "Well, it's about time!" Jennifer thought. They have only been together since forever, it seemed.

The posting was a few days old so thankfully Jennifer still had time to send them a congratulatory message. The announcement declared that the wedding was to be at the end of May in Cocoa Beach, Florida. The couple had been living there since Ethan graduated with an advanced degree in aeronautics and went to work with NASA. In lieu of formal invitations, since there was nothing formal about Jacy nor Ethan, the Facebook announcement was also serving as the wedding invitation. Any friends and family that could make it should reply to the posting. "Well, that's certainly a modern approach." Jennifer grinned as she knew it was typical of the couple to be that nonchalant about their own wedding.

After clicking the "Like" icon and commenting a quick "Congrats!" Jennifer noticed she had messages. There were five messages from Jacy. The bride-to-be was curious why Jennifer never answered her home phone and why didn't she have voicemail. The next message scolded her for not keeping in touch and providing her friends current contact information as she was desperate to talk to her sorority big sister and best friend. Another message instructed Jennifer to call her STAT because she had a very important question to ask her. Looking at the clock, she realized it probably wasn't too early to call so she picked up her phone to dial the number listed in the last message.

A groggy Ethan answered the phone but was more than delighted to disturb his soon-to-be wife who was already awake and had just returned from walking the dogs. Jacy's squeal of delight nearly ruptured Jennifer's eardrum. After letting Jacy run on for several minutes about the upcoming wedding and lecturing her friend on her lack of manners for not staying in touch, she excitedly asked the burning question... "Jennifer, will you be my maid of honor?" This was followed by more declarations that she HAD to be her maid of honor and she was NOT taking no for an answer. Typical Jacy.

Promising to check her schedule and to get back to her later that day, Jennifer ended the call hoping she would not have to disappoint Jacy but uneasy with the thought of attending a wedding. Her own personal life was, well lacking the personal part. She was not a big socialite, even though the Chief of Pediatric Oncology enjoyed forcing her to attend fund raisers to benefit the hospital whenever he saw fit. Social settings were just not her thing.

Jennifer noticed another message in her inbox. This time from a blast from the past male friend, also from college, Lorenzo Esposito. Now what could he want? They hadn't spoken to each other since graduation. Despite being close friends in those days, she realized she didn't even know what his post-grad plans entailed. Although they had hung out quite often, going to sporting events together and the occasional party, Jennifer had been too busy trying to get into medical school and Lorenzo chasing skirts around campus for anything more to ever develop between them. Friends had teased that they should stop trying to fool everyone because they obviously belonged together.

She and Lorenzo would just laugh it off with a mischievous wink at each other. Never had anything other than a platonic "just friends" relationship ever entered their minds.

Curious what Lorenzo had to say after so many years, Jennifer clicked on the message. It was short and sweet. The usual, "Hi, how are you? I'm fine. Long time, no see." He had heard about the wedding and Ethan had asked him to be the best man but he was lacking a date to the event. Even though they had not kept in touch he was hopeful she would save him from having to RSVP as "1". He went on to explain that he was uncomfortable taking a "date" since weddings were seen as either the kiss of death for a relationship or as getting in line to be the next sucker down the aisle. He could do without the hassle either way. Lorenzo went on to note that he noticed her scant profile on Facebook as showing she was still unattached so he was pleading once again for her help, just like the good ole days in college. He needed a no-frills, no-strings attached wedding date and was hoping she would agree. "Wow! What a romantic?!" she thought sarcastically. He ended the message with his contact information if she was interested in helping him out.

Signing out of Facebook without responding, Jennifer took up her now tepid coffee and thought back to the outgoing, charismatic, undeniably handsome man Lorenzo had been in college. Tall, dark, and handsome didn't come close to describing him then. For a moment she allowed herself to imagine what he might look like now years later. She had to admit, the picture in her head was nice...very nice, indeed. Throughout college Lorenzo had always attracted the ladies, in droves. At one point their group of friends had taken to calling him "Casanova" because of his love'em and leave'em attitude.

After college the gang had all gone their separate ways. Jennifer had been horrible about keeping in contact with anyone. However, she did remotely recall Jacy mentioning that Lorenzo had married a woman he met at his first job after graduation. Jennifer had been surprised the mighty Casanova had fallen so soon. It must not have worked out if he was hitting her up for a wedding date.

While heading out the door to the hospital, she promised herself to clear her schedule at work so she could attend her friend's wedding. Besides she had not taken time off from the hospital in all her years working there. Not even for holidays to go visit her folks in Denver. She was due some R&R and this was the perfect excuse. As soon as she cleared the time off with her boss, she would contact Lorenzo.

After making her rounds at the hospital later that day, Jennifer sought out the Chief of Pediatric Oncology, Jacob Mallory, to discuss her "vacation". She found him where she expected to find him...on the phone in his office attempting to drum up more money for the department from a donor. He motioned for her to take a seat while he wrapped up the call. Jacob was not just the chief of her department but she also considered him a friend. He was of average height but built like a linebacker. His physique was always displayed at its best in Armani or other designer suits with his dark blonde hair cut short and always clean-shaven. Outside of the hospital environment he could easily be mistaken for one of the bigwigs up on Capitol Hill. He was equally suited to the political life. After all, wining and dining for cash from the elites was his specialty.

Ending his call, he turned his piercing aqua blue eyes on her with a charming grin meant to make her melt but somehow she never felt the impact of his bedroom eyes. They briefly discussed her current case load and results of some tests she was running on a new patient. She hoped the prescribed protocol would work since the cancer seemed to be caught in the early stages. The results were still being validated but Jennifer was optimistic. After a few minutes she got up the courage to voice her request.

Looking somewhat shocked, but pleasantly surprised, Jacob reassured her that vacation time was much overdue for the workaholic doctor. However, he added that he would be delighted to go with her.

Jennifer knew that was a danger area. She had attended some hospital fundraising functions with Jacob and knew he was attracted to her but she had no desire to complicate their relationship. Declining with the excuse of spending time with old friends, she thanked him as she rose from the uncomfortable office armchair to attend to the remainder of her day.

Later that evening, Jennifer returned to her snug condo with a large brown paper bag filled with several containers from the corner Chinese restaurant. Not realizing until much too late that she had not eaten at all during the day, she was ravenous by the time she headed home. Not even bothering to transfer the food from the take-out containers to a plate, she dove into the combination fried rice first. After satiating her hunger and fixing a cup of jasmine tea, she sat back down in her favorite armchair and pulled her computer onto her lap.

First, she notified Jacy that she would indeed attend the wedding and be her maid of honor. Luckily, Jacy was so laid back that she allowed Jennifer to pick out her own dress, as long as it was lavender in color. "Terrific," she thought, "purple does nothing for my Irish freckled complexion." Next, she composed a short message to Lorenzo stating she would attend the wedding and would also appreciate a "no strings" date. They could arrange to meet up once they both got to Cocoa Beach. Before signing off the computer, Jennifer booked her flight, a rental car, and her suite at the resort where Jacy and Ethan would be married.

Following a hot shower and veg'ing out to some reality television show for an hour, Jennifer retired for the night. The wedding had given her something else to think about aside from her young patients awaiting a miracle cure. Jennifer briefly entertained the hope that tonight her sleep would not be interrupted by nightmares. Maybe there would instead be images of warm sands and the sound of relaxing waves and a tall, dark, and handsome man.

The wedding approached quickly and Jennifer left a muggy Washington, DC over Memorial Day weekend for the hot and humid climate of the Central Atlantic Florida coast. In the last few months she had managed to grow her strawberry-blonde locks out just past her shoulders, and had even gone in for a professional mani-pedi a couple hours before her flight. A friend from the hospital had taken her shopping for a dress suitable for the occasion. Despite the lavender not being her best shade, Jennifer was surprised she was actually happy with the selection. She was not happy with the 2 inch high heels they had selected though. She hadn't worn heels since medical school graduation. However, they were necessary as her dress was long and her legs were short.

After a short plane ride and an even shorter drive from Orlando to Cocoa Beach, Jennifer arrived at The Cocoa Sands Resort and Spa shortly before the wedding rehearsal. If she was lucky, she would have a chance to stroll on the beach before meeting everyone in the ballroom. Luck was not to be had as Jacy spotted her friend in the lobby and rushed over to hug and greet her. Jacy was still the same as in college. Super model gorgeous with long legs and shining long blonde hair. She took charge of the situation and sent the bell hop to the room with Jennifer's luggage while she dragged the weary traveler to the outdoor bar area where everyone else had already congregated.

Seeing some familiar faces and some not-so familiar faces, Jennifer was handed a drink while making introductions and greeting old friends. Not all of the old gang was here, it seemed. She would have to ask Jacy about that later since she was being reprimanded for being the last to arrive by Jacy's mom. Through the crowd, at the other end of the bar, sat a very familiar handsome face – Lorenzo. The groom immediately piped up that he was just glad his buddy's date had finally shown up because it was a shame for such a man to be all alone. "Oh no!" Jennifer thought. She had heard this line of discussion before quite a number of times during college. Anytime Lorenzo had been girlfriend-free for more than five minutes, Ethan and Jacy had pushed them to get together. Maybe agreeing to this wedding date was a mistake.

There wasn't a lot of time for conversation as the wedding planner came out to the bar to escort the wedding party into the ballroom for rehearsal. Jennifer could tell this lady ran a tight ship and thrived on the stress of producing the perfect wedding for her clients. Considering how laid back Jacy and Ethan were about such thing, they had waited several years to tie the knot officially after all, Jennifer was surprised in their pick for a wedding planner. Guess it was better for someone else to stress about the wedding because the bride and groom weren't going to do so. As they were walking back into the hotel, Jennifer felt a soft touch on her elbow. Turning around she gazed up at her incredibly tall, incredibly attractive, wedding date. Lorenzo always had the most amazing smile and it was in full force as he linked their arms together to usher her into the ballroom. The warmth from his touch was reassuring and familiar as he had escorted her to a dozen or more functions in college. "Yes," she thought, "This was a good idea." Wordlessly they entered the ballroom with the rest of the party and took their respective places.

The rehearsal, thankfully, was short and sweet. Jennifer was ravenous since once again she had forgotten to eat that day. A full seven course meal awaited everyone in the main banquet hall of the resort. The tables were littered with place cards with centerpieces of fragrant candles and rose petals. She was looking forward to the meal and getting reacquainted with Lorenzo, as well as other long lost friends from the good ole days. Engaged in conversation with Janice, another former college friend who had always been known as the "mother" of the group, Jennifer felt someone staring at her. Looking around she discovered two of the darkest, most gorgeous chocolate brown eyes gazing at her from across the room. Lorenzo had already found their designated places and had her chair pulled out for her.

Mumbling an excuse to Janice, Jennifer began to walk over to him realizing she was being way too self-conscious about herself as she neared him, with her head slightly bowed but looking up through her lush brown eye lashes shielding brilliant emerald green eyes. "Why am I so nervous?" she thought with some frustration.

The dinner was superb and the conversation flowed easily around the table full of college pals. Janice was married with a passel of kids, all under the age of eight which were at home in Pennsylvania with her husband. Kyle had his own architectural firm in Dallas and had just become engaged to his assistant Sarah. He assured everyone that they were invited to the nuptials next winter. Candace was a divorced nurse and single mom but was hoping her boyfriend of the last three years would finally pop the question. He responded with a flamboyant roll of his eyes. Everyone was in good health and good spirits. It truly was fantastic to be back with her group of friends. Until now Jennifer had not realized just how much she had missed them. Her world now consisted of work, work, and more work. No friends really outside of the hospital and definitely no boyfriend.

Lorenzo, however, remained quiet as everyone else discussed their lives since college and plans for the future. Jennifer didn't remember him being the quiet one. He was always the jovial, fun all the time, type of guy. He would offer a small smile or laugh as appropriate, but seemed to be staying outside the conversation instead of a part of it. His silence unnerved her but she didn't wish to ask unwanted questions but made a mental note to ask Jacy about the alteration in Lorenzo later.

With dinner over, the wedding party moved back to the outdoor bar area where they could enjoy the cool ocean breeze and their drinks. Not realizing just how tired she was, and there wasn't nearly enough food in her stomach to combat much more alcohol, Jennifer chose a lounge chair by the pool to relax in. At least she could kick off her strappy high heel sandals she had been in all day. Her feet were going to really hurt tomorrow. Jennifer had worn nothing but sneakers and crocs since graduating medical school. She was not cut out for heels, despite the need for added height, as she barely topped out at 5'2". Everyone else gathered around the pool deck, sipping mai tai's and other fruity umbrella drinks. Ethan started the group on something he called zombie brain shots. She didn't know what was in it but it looked disgusting. Jennifer declined. With that the party was in full swing. Good thing the wedding ceremony wasn't until late afternoon tomorrow as this particular group was going to need some hangover recovery time in the morning.

The party lasted well into the evening but most began to file away to their respective rooms shortly after midnight. Jennifer had nearly fallen asleep in her lounge chair. It wasn't until the last of the chattering died away that she noticed she was alone except for Lorenzo who had taken up a perch along the side of the pool, splashing his feet around. Throughout the after-dinner party, he had still remained quiet. This was not the man she remembered from college. The larger-than-life sexy, fun-loving Casanova. This made her sad and want to find out what was bothering her friend. Yes, they had been out of touch for many years. However, she found that she still cared about his well-being and had missed his presence in her life all this time. She got up from her lounge chair and walked over to the pool to sit down beside him. For several moments, they just sat there without saying a word.

Lorenzo was the first to break the awkward silence between them by remarking about being proud she had realized her dream of being a prominent pediatric doctor in a renowned hospital. It was a vague attempt at small talk. She thanked him and then they sat in silence for a while longer until Jennifer couldn't bare it anymore. Turning to him and looking up into his eyes, she saw sorrow reflected in their dark pools. There was an overwhelming desire to just hug him tightly as if he needed a shoulder to cry on. The urge was so strong that she did timidly reach up to stroke his cheek, which was prickly from a day or two old growth of beard. Instead of withdrawing from her as she feared, he placed his hand over hers and held it for what seemed many moments with his eyes closed. "La mia bella amica," he uttered softly.

After sitting a few more moments in silence, Lorenzo turned to Jennifer with that old familiar smile she was accustomed to seeing. "I'm so sorry for being such a poor date. It wasn't what I planned at all. I thought the wedding would be a good distraction for me and instead I've only been sad since arriving here. That's no way to treat such a beautiful lady," he said with sincerity. She could tell he was sad but didn't understand why.

Jennifer gazed up into his eyes and said softly, "I'll forgive you but you have to tell me why you are so sad. I was expecting this larger than life happy-go-lucky dude from my youth. Seeing you this way makes me sad and worried. This 'date' as you call it can only get better but you have to be straight with me."

With that he sighed and let the tale spill out. He had married several years ago to a wonderful woman, Lisa. They were happy and even happier when they became a family with the birth of their son Raphael. A spirited five year old that was a miniature version of himself with his wife's quirky sense of humor. Their happiness was cut short a couple years back when Lisa was killed in a horrific accident on I-66 coming home from work one day. She wasn't even supposed to be on the roads but had offered to deliver company documents to the Senate sub-planning committee chairman since he and his business partner were overwhelmed completing a project for another client.

Lorenzo continued his story about how he was struggling as a single dad. Business was fine but he worried about his son growing up without his mom. If he had to admit it, he was also lonely and missed his wife very much. He thought he'd brave it out for Ethan and Jacy by coming to the wedding but it was taking more of a toll on him than he had imagined. That was why he had sent her the Facebook message. He knew if anyone could see him through this weekend, it would be Jennifer. "Guess I should've been more upfront and explained all that beforehand. Quite frankly I never thought you'd say yes. Figured you had some hot shot doctor boyfriend to escort you here." With that last statement he actually conjured up a small teasing half-smile.

Jennifer continued to hold his hand and listen for hours as he told stories about his wife and his son. He took out his iPhone to show her a picture and the boy was indeed a copy of his handsome dad. Their conversation flowed to other topics such as her career and lack of a personal life, what they had been up to since college, and reminiscing about their time together in school. Before they realized it the sun was coming up over the ocean horizon and they were still seated on the pool deck with their feet dangling in the water.

As the hotel staff was starting about their day, Lorenzo and Jennifer went to their own rooms for much needed rest. Despite no sleep since the day before, her head was spinning with everything he had told her. After getting through all the sadness, they had reconnected during the course of the night. Felt like she had her friend back and with that thought she was able to close her eyes and sleep.

A few hours later a loud banging awoke her. She had overslept. It was Jacy with the brilliant smile of a happy bride. The two women exchanged stories as Jennifer jumped in the shower and got ready for the day. Thankfully, the wedding planner had arranged for someone to do their make-up and hair. All she had to do was make herself presentable. While waiting on her friend, Jacy took pleasure teasing Jennifer about her late night sojourn with Lorenzo. Jacy had always hoped the two would end up together, ever since their freshman days. They had thwarted every attempt by herself and Ethan to make the transition from friends to lovers. Secretly, Jacy wished that her wedding might light a fire in their direction but she kept that information to herself.

A few hours later, after a quick brunch, getting dolled up by the resort's spa staff, and getting the bride squeezed into her lacy, halter-top styled wedding gown, it was time. Jacy didn't seem nervous at all. She and Ethan had been together so long the wedding was just a formality. Jennifer, on the other hand, felt shaky as she proceeded down the carpeted aisle from the pool area to a spot on the beach where the groom and his handsome best man awaited. Traversing the terrain in high heels had been a bad idea after all. She nervously glanced up as she approached them and saw Lorenzo smiling at her with a gleam in his eyes. She gave him a quick wink and stepped aside for the bride's arrival, trying her best not to trip.

The wedding was short and simple. No frills but still sweet and romantic. Within minutes Jacy and Ethan were pronounced husband and wife, kissed, and everyone cheered. Jennifer glanced over to see how Lorenzo was handling the situation. She needn't have worried. He was all smiles and staring straight at her. Her stomach experienced an unfamiliar butterfly sensation, but she dismissed it in her mind as needing to eat something. "It couldn't be more than that," she thought. The reception was held in the ballroom with French doors that opened out to the beach area. During dinner Lorenzo gave a sincere, yet hilarious toast to the bride and groom as he regaled the wedding guests with the story of how the two had met, had instantly despised each other, but within a week were caught making out in the chem lab. Everyone laughed, except Jacy's parents. It was her turn. Jennifer had forgotten she needed to make a toast so she tried to wing it. After stumbling around for the right words, she went with the traditional congratulatory message to the groom with best wishes for the bride. Then reversed herself saying "Knowing Jacy as well as I do, maybe the best wishes part belongs to the groom. Hope you have a big enough closet for all her shoes and that you don't live near an animal shelter since Jacy will bring home every single dog, cat, bird, mouse, whatever."

Music began shortly afterwards and the dance party ensued. Jacy and Ethan had always been big dancers and had dragged Jennifer and Lorenzo to all the clubs around campus. Jennifer was never comfortable in that environment, but Lorenzo always seemed to make it okay. Just like old times, he stayed by her side the entire night and didn't pull her out onto the dance floor until a Frank Sinatra ballad began to play. He didn't even ask. Just took her arm and led her out to dance. She recognized the strains of "The Way You Look Tonight". Lorenzo was the only person who understood her preference for Frank Sinatra over Nirvana. It had been a running joke that Jennifer had arrived at campus in a time capsule from the 1950s because she never liked the typical "alternative" music most co-eds did.

They danced closely. For some reason Jennifer couldn't find the courage to look up into his eyes. All she could focus on was the feel of his hand stroking the small of her back through the flimsy dress material as they danced and listening to the beat of his heart as she laid her head on his chest. If they were back in school they would be bantering back and forth about who was the better dancer or just joking around in general.

Too soon the song ended to be replaced by "The Chicken Dance". Hoping to escape, Jennifer pulled away to walk back to the sidelines but Lorenzo had other ideas. Yes, she was going to have to endure this most ridiculous wedding ritual. She was sure the "Electric Slide" would follow soon enough, but hoped they had seen fit to exclude "The Macarena". Before realizing it, it had been several upbeat dance numbers and she was still on the dance floor. Sweaty and thirsty, she motioned to Lorenzo that she was getting a drink. He followed closely behind as they grabbed a couple champagne flutes off a nearby waiter's tray and strolled outside for a breath of fresh air.

Removing her shoes on the sand, they walked out to the edge of the Atlantic Ocean. The sun was setting over the horizon. Jennifer plopped down on the sand to take in the beauty of the scene as she rarely saw the sunset anymore since she was always at the hospital or in the lab. Lorenzo joined her as they silently watched the glowing orange orb seemingly descend into the water. It was the first time in years that either of them had felt peaceful. This weekend had done wonders for them both, whether they realized it or not.

Unaware of the passage of time, the bride and groom came searching for them an hour later for the bouquet and garter throwing tradition. Jennifer always tried to make herself scarce during this particular portion of any wedding but decided to humor Jacy this once. Luckily, one of the groom's sisters was intent on being the next to get hitched and knocked everyone out of the way. Lorenzo stood stock still as Ethan threw the garter right at him and let the item fall to the floor where the pre-teen ring bearer grabbed it up. With all the wedding traditions complete, the bride and groom quickly made their exit so they could start the real celebrations in the honeymoon suite. The rest of the wedding party meandered around the ballroom for a while longer but started to disperse for their own rooms. Jennifer looked over at Lorenzo with a coy smile and motioned for him to follow her.

Earlier that day Jennifer had spotted a billiards room down the hall from the spa area. In college they had played pool against each other relentlessly. A few times they had partnered up to swindle money from unsuspecting underclassmen. With a wink, she began to rack up the balls and selected her cue stick. "How about a friendly wager? For old times' sake," she challenged.

Laughing, Lorenzo accepted her dare. After requesting a couple drinks from the bartender, he asked, "So what are we betting this time? It's not like I have a research paper I need your help on anymore and I don't think they will allow me on the plane with a case of scotch. What's it gonna be, little girl?"

"Alright there, jolly green giant," she teased back with the pet name she had given him freshman year, "We're both relatively successful people. We could actually bet real money this time."

With a frown, he replied, "No. No. That's no fun. Let's make it interesting. Whoever wins gets to make the other either tell a truth or take a dare." This proposal had potential but Jennifer was a little wary recalling past dares from him but decided to just go with it.

"You're on, big guy," she retorted with a smirk. Even though she hadn't played pool in years she was confidant it would come back to her. However, the strategy didn't work quite as she had planned. After thoroughly whipping his opponent, not once but three separate times, Jennifer admitted defeat and pleaded for mercy.

Appearing deep in thought Lorenzo issued his ultimatum. Truth or dare? Always uncomfortable with the truth category, she chose "dare". His dark eyes sparkled at the prospect as he contemplated his request. "Okay, I dare you to skinny dip in the pool or ocean right now."

Thankfully the alcohol that had flowed all night helped her find courage to do so but she was still not happy about it. After trying several times to convince Lorenzo to go "Best 5 out of 7 games", she resigned herself to her fate. Even the bartender snickered as she headed out to the door to the pool. After seeing that the pool was a bit too well lit for her liking, she chose the darker, more concealing ocean. Jennifer timidly approached the edge of the surf to test the water temperature before shedding any clothes. Being the Atlantic Ocean, it was chilly no matter what time of year.

Looking back to see Lorenzo standing smugly a few yards back, Jennifer instructed him to turn around and close his eyes. Despite it being nighttime, the moon was full and cast too much light on the beach for her liking. Grumbling under her breath that she should have known not to accept a dare from that man in particular, she tried the zipper at the back of the dress. It wouldn't budge. After a number of failed attempts she gave up and called for Lorenzo to help. The look on his face said that he was enjoying this a bit too much. He unhooked the clasp at the top, which she had completely forgotten about, and then slowly slid the zipper down to the small of her back. Her skin was chilled from the cool breeze coming off the ocean but where his fingers barely grazed her back as he worked the zipper almost seemed on fire. She shook her head slightly to clear her head. "Must be the alcohol affecting me," she reasoned.

With the zipper situation remedied, Lorenzo retreated to his spot on the sand a few yards away. Being a gentleman, he turned away as she undressed. Still in her undies, Jennifer started to enter the water when she heard, "Skinny dipping means skin only, little girl," followed by a smug chuckle. Wincing at being caught trying to cheat, she shed the rest of her garments and plunged into the waves.

Resurfacing quickly she looked over to see Lorenzo doubled over laughing. Wishing to get out of the frigid water and avoid any ocean inhabitants, she tersely instructed him to get a towel or at least turn around while she put her clothes back on. He turned away still laughing. As she came onshore she couldn't find her undies. In her haste she had discarded them too close to the edge of the water and they had floated away with the tide. Reaching for her dress, Jennifer realized that due to being thoroughly drenched, she had difficulty getting it back on. After a few minutes struggling, Lorenzo had finally ceased laughing and questioned what was taking so long. Embarrassed she admitted the truth causing more laughter to erupt. After a few seconds, she started laughing too at the ridiculousness of a thirty-something year old doctor childishly taking a silly dare to strip off her clothes and run into the ocean. Her present predicament with the dress just highlighted the hilarity of the situation.

Finally regaining his composure, Lorenzo backed over to her so as not to see her clinging to the flimsy dress. He had left his suit jacket in the billiard room so he unbuttoned his dress shirt and handed it to her. Being so tall and Jennifer being so short, the shirt covered her almost to her knees. Playfully hitting him in the chest with the crumbled up dress, they made their way back to the hotel.

Luckily, due to the lateness of the hour, the lobby and hallways were relatively empty. Lorenzo escorted her back to her room. They were both still giggling when they arrived at her door. As she turned to open the door, Jennifer found herself wanting to invite him in for a drink but thought better of it. Instead she thanked him for a memorable "date" and gave him a quick kiss on cheek before retreating into her suite and closing the door behind her. She stood with her back against the door for several moments contemplating why she had gotten so nervous just now. It was just Lorenzo after all.

Jennifer practically snuck out of the hotel the next morning to leave for the airport. Not sure why she didn't want to run into anyone, particularly Lorenzo, she was packed and driving away almost before the resort starting serving breakfast. She wasn't the only one attempting to escape unnoticed. As she entered the airport lobby she spotted his tall, dark head of hair at the check-in counter. The silly, flirty looks the airline attendant was giving him made Jennifer roll her eyes. Lorenzo could always turn seemingly normal women into acting like gaga teenagers drooling over him. In college it had been entertaining to watch. Now, she was just annoyed.

Momentarily he turned around and caught her staring at him. Flashing that swoon-worthy smile he walked over on the pretense of helping with her luggage. "Hope you remembered my shirt when you packed this morning," he joked. They compared airline itineraries and discovered they were on the same flight to Reagan National. Appearing happy about the situation, Lorenzo proceeded through the line with her to the check-in counter where he requested a seat change for her so they could sit together in first class. The same attendant as before did not seem thrilled to fulfill his request. Jennifer stifled a giggle as the woman banged away on her computer terminal to make the switch.

They had plenty of time to stroll to the concourse as the flight wasn't for another two hours. Lorenzo suggested stopping for coffee and muffins. Jennifer agreed to the coffee. "Are you still not eating breakfast? No wonder you are so tiny," he remarked. Two tall vanilla lattes later, they were seated in the terminal with nothing to say. In silence they sipped their coffees and stared out the window waiting on their flight to arrive.

Finally, Lorenzo broke the silence by saying, "Listen. You know my situation and I know yours. Neither of us is looking for a relationship, but I really do miss your friendship. I was kind of hoping we could keep in touch more, especially now that we know we live in the same metro area. Also, we could help each other out of awkward situations, like going to weddings or events without the stress of someone thinking it was a real date." Jennifer nodded her head in agreement and looked up into his chocolate eyes. Having a sexy standby, go-to date was the perfect solution. She stuck her hand out to shake his to seal the agreement, but he leaned in and gave her a quick peck on the cheek.

The return flight went quickly as they discussed a myriad of topics. He spoke mostly about his son and his genetically-inherited love of soccer. She discussed her work at the hospital and how she wished she had more time for research since she felt a big breakthrough was just around the corner. Before they knew it, the fasten seatbelts sign lit up and the airplane descended. Having the window seat, Jennifer always enjoyed the arrival into this particular airport as it gave the illusion that the plane was about to crash into the Potomac River right before landing safely on the thin strip of land.

After retrieving their luggage, Jennifer made to give him a swift goodbye hug. Instead she found herself in a giant bear hug. Neither really wanted to let go. Saying goodbye, they headed their separate ways. Lorenzo to the parking garage to drive back to the DC suburb of Warrenton, VA. Jennifer to the Metro station to take the train into the District.

Jennifer's thoughts remained on Lorenzo the entire ride back to the station closest to her Georgetown condo. It was a long walk from there in the humid weather with the clouds overhead, threatening rain. She didn't notice though. Her mind ran over the events of the past couple days. Never in the last few years had she allowed herself to daydream. She was just too busy for that. Nevertheless, as a spattering of rain drops began to fall Jennifer didn't even notice as she replayed the Sinatra song dance over and over in her mind. She blushed at the memory of her skinny dipping escapade. But the image that kept asserting itself was of Lorenzo smiling wickedly at her as they played pool. Her skin still felt the faint trace of where his fingers had brushed against her back unzipping her dress. Perhaps agreeing to be each other's go-to wedding date had not been the greatest idea.

Jennifer resumed her normal schedule and didn't hear from Lorenzo for a couple of weeks. Trying to justify her increased interest in Facebook, she lied to herself that she wasn't really just seeing if there were any messages from him. She was genuinely interested in everyone's pet pictures and what they had for dinner. Then one stormy evening as she was relaxing after a long day at the hospital with a cup of herbal tea and a bowl of sugary kids' cereal, her Facebook page finally indicated she had a message. Surprisingly, she could feel her heart beating faster in her chest when she saw that it was indeed from Lorenzo with an apology for not contacting her sooner. He indicated that he wasn't really comfortable communicating via social media and requested her number instead, or at least a viable email account. He included his full contact information in the message so she took out her cell phone and plugged in his information after sending a quick reply with her own information.

Later that night as she was just getting out of the shower the phone rang. No one ever called her except the hospital so she assumed it was the dreaded "There's a patient in distress" or worse call. Without glancing at the caller id, she answered and was delighted to hear the deep, husky voice of Lorenzo. Jennifer was surprised he called her so soon after she sent her contact information. Still wearing a towel and her hair dripping wet, she sat down on her bed to chat.

Hours later she was still wearing a towel with her hair dried naturally wavy and tousled. They had talked about everything and nothing, it seemed. When Jennifer happened to glance over at the clock she was shocked to see it was well past midnight. As she tried to say goodbye, Lorenzo surprised her again by stating there was a particular reason for his call. He needed a date. His son's teacher was getting married. His son really wanted to go to the wedding, but Lorenzo dreaded the matchmaking that would go on if he showed up without a female companion. Every one of Raphael's teachers and room moms seemed to make setting him up with any available female in the school district as their personal goal in life. He hated it! "Please, please, pretty please," he begged, "save me from this impending disaster!" Laughing at his predicament, she tried to play coy with her answer just to tease him. Ultimately showing pity, Jennifer agreed. She wrote down the date and time on her whiteboard in the kitchen and made a mental note to double check her schedule at work. Jokingly thanking her for saving his life, he said good night. Once she hung up the phone, doubt set in. Not only was she going to another wedding with him. She was also going there with his son. Jennifer wished she had thought of that before saying "yes".

As it turned out, she wasn't scheduled to work the day in question so no backing out that way. Her supervisor, Jacob, was somewhat taken aback when he later asked her to attend a hospital fundraising event at the Mayflower Hotel that same evening. Teasing her about finally getting a social life, he mildly suggested that he hoped she still had time for her research. The comment was completely uncalled for but had its intended effect by making Jennifer doubt herself. "Was it really necessary that she spend her time helping out an old friend, who quite frankly should be getting set up on dates in order to meet someone and provide a mother-figure for Raphael," she thought. "Perhaps it was selfish of her to want to spend time away from the hospital or anything benefitting the hospital when saving children's lives with her research was the most important thing in the world." After mulling it over, she had almost convinced herself to cancel with Lorenzo. However, when she tried to call him to tell him so, he sounded so excited and grateful she was going to be there with him that Jennifer didn't have the heart to turn him down.

Not having a car since living in DC, on the date of the teacher's wedding, she took the Metro to the subway station farthest west of the city. Lorenzo would pick her up there. To avoid walking the many blocks to the Metro station in painful high heels, she slipped her comfy sneakers on and packed the heels away in an oversized designer purse her mother had given her for Christmas. The vision of a petite woman in a pale green sundress and sneakers must have been amusing because Lorenzo starting chuckling as soon as he saw her emerge from the station. "Cut it out, meathead, or I'm turning around and getting back on that train," she threatened.

"Hey, Dad! You going to let her get away with calling you that?" said a robust little boy voice. Lorenzo was so tall she hadn't even seen the little boy behind him. He was a perfect miniature of his father with dark olive skin and jet black hair that was a little too long and kept falling over his large, almond-shaped eyes. He was dressed in a khaki pants, with a button-down shirt and even a clip on tie. The perfect little man, except for the dirt-smudged sneakers on his feet. "My kind of kid," she thought. She wondered how much Lorenzo had argued with the boy to get him in the dress clothes.

Lorenzo laughed and replied, "Yes, I will let it slip this once since she is a lady and we should always show them respect." With that he introduced his son and the little man reached out to shake her hand. Being a little Casanova himself, the boy adeptly turned her hand so he could bend over to kiss the top. Jennifer thanked him and complimented him on his attire and manners. He, in turn, commented on her brand of sneakers since apparently they were not the "in" brand of his generation. As the two continued to debate the finer aspects of various sneaker brands, Lorenzo escorted them back to the car.

To say Raphael was charming was indeed an understatement. He entertained Jennifer the entire ride to the church where the wedding was to take place. She was so captivated by him she forgot to change her shoes in the car. As she stepped out of Lorenzo's white Chevy SUV, he made a little "hmm hmm" noise. When she looked up at him oblivious to the problem, he started laughing. This time Raphael jumped in to scold his father for laughing at a lady. After thanking her little hero, she finally noticed the issue and started laughing herself. This seemed to confuse the boy. After his brave defense of the pretty lady, she was now laughing. When she sat back down in the car and pulled out her high heels to change he was even more shocked. How could one explain to a five year old boy that he could get away with wearing sneakers to a wedding but a lady could not? Raphael just rolled his eyes and said "Whatever".

As they walked arm in arm towards the church, Jennifer admired her escort out of the corner of her eye. Lorenzo looked dapper in a light grey suit and plum colored silk tie. His hair had grown longer since the wedding in Cocoa Beach and fell over his right eye hiding a small scar just below his eye brow. Jennifer recalled him explaining the scar to her one night. When he was ten years old, an opposing team player was angry at losing a game and in the last second of the game kicked the ball as hard as he could right at Lorenzo's face, splitting the skin above his eye. Just before walking into the church, she reached up to brush the hair away from his eyes and unconsciously allowed her finger to lightly trace the scar.

As soon as they entered Jennifer felt that all eyes were on them. At least all the females in the room were looking at Lorenzo and sizing her up. He may not realize it but she could tell some of those females weren't too happy to see another woman on his arm. Lorenzo, on the other hand, saw more than a few envious stares from the attending men. He knew he had a hottie on his arm and he enjoyed the satisfaction of knowing that this fetching beauty was with him. Just friends or not, he was still proud to be seen with Jennifer whether she was in sneakers, a formal dress, or just his shirt. The image of her wearing his shirt coming off the beach had haunted him ever since that night. Attempting to shake off the vision, as they were in a church and that could only lead to "un-churchly" thoughts, he moved to shake hands with some of the gentlemen in the foyer and to introduce his date.

They were ushered into the crowded sanctuary by an elderly gentlemen and took their places in a middle row. Luckily the ceremony started soon after their arrival as Jennifer was feeling awkward having so many people looking her over She knew they were evaluating in their minds if she was good enough for the handsome man next to her. Some, she noticed, frowned. Others gave a small grin of approval. However, there was more than one that gave her an outright evil look. The buxom blonde in the third row was obviously not happy with her presence. Sweet-natured Raphael kept leaning over to point out and whisper the names of everyone he knew. The blonde in question was the teacher's assistant in his class.

The ceremony was beautiful and much longer and formal than Jacy's wedding had been. Raphael was well-mannered and remained quiet and observant the entire time. Too bad the three preteens in the back row weren't so well-mannered. When the ceremony was over, they went back to the car to drive to the local country club for the reception. Raphael resumed his constant chatter with Jennifer. He pointed out his school and his team's soccer practice field. He described, in detail, his last game where he scored the winning goal against his arch rival Landon. The boy definitely had spunk and character. Jennifer already loved him and they had only been together for an hour or more.

The reception was held at an antebellum-looking house overlooking a pristine golf course. There were tennis courts adjacent to the building and a pool with colorful winding slides behind it. After dinner the children were taken to another room in the building where they could play arcade games or use the indoor basketball courts while the adults stayed in the banquet hall for dancing and drinks. Several people came over to introduce themselves, including the teacher/bride. One sweet middle-aged woman, who had already had a bit too much wine with dinner, commented that Raphael's dad had outdone himself with his date and that she shouldn't mind the other women there giving her jealous stares. Laughing, Jennifer agreed wholeheartedly. However, she was shocked when the blonde teacher assistant strutted over, and without acknowledging Jennifer's presence, asked Lorenzo to dance.

He was stunned as well and indicated he already promised his date a dance. With that, he led Jennifer to the small dance floor as the music changed from some hip-hop number to a more subdued soft rock ballad. Trying not to giggle, Jennifer glanced over at the blonde woman who had stormed off.

The rest of the evening, Lorenzo and Jennifer kept mostly to themselves. Dancing when it was a slow tune and sitting out the club dance music. Raphael came bounding into the room again when he tired of the game room. Deciding it was time to leave, they again congratulated the bride and groom and made a beeline out the door. Once outside, Lorenzo issued a genuine sigh of relief it was over. Jennifer now understood why he had needed her tonight – to fend off the hordes of women wanting to throw themselves at him. "Must be a tough life," she thought as she started to giggle. Raphael just looked confused. He was so cute at that moment, Jennifer had to resist the urge to pinch his little cheeks. She was pretty sure he would not appreciate that.

The little boy seemed genuinely upset when they arrived back at the Metro station for Jennifer to catch her ride home. Looking into his sad face, so much like his father's, she promised it would not be the last time they would see each other. Surprising even herself, she asked him for a hug which he gladly provided. The look on Lorenzo's face as she shyly glanced up through her eye lashes, was a mixture of sadness and pride. Jennifer imagined he would give anything to have Raphael's mother here to give him hugs. Standing on tiptoe, as she had quickly reclaimed the sneakers when they had left the reception so was lacking the added height from the heels, she gave Lorenzo a quick kiss on the cheek while holding onto his hand so as not to topple from the effort. Being so tall, she was truly on the tips of her toes. He, in turn, held the tips of her fingers a little than necessary as if not wanting to let go. With a reassuring smile, Jennifer turned towards the Metro station to leave.

Lorenzo sent a thank you message to her via Facebook the next day with an emoticon of flowers. After that, Jennifer didn't hear from him for over a week. She tried to convince herself she wasn't disappointed and refocused all her energies on her patients.

A new protocol she had designed was showing positive results for a couple of her younger patients in the earlier cancer stages. Unfortunately, it had been too little too late for one young boy in the more advanced stages of lymphoma. It had been an incredibly difficult day as she dealt with his loss. Jennifer kept chastising herself for not developing the protocol sooner so she could've saved him. Jacob, after seeing her distress, ordered her to take the rest of the day off. Several hours were spent running to rid herself of her demons. The ones that tormented her every time she lost a patient.

She heard her phone ringing as she approached the door to her condo. Unable to unlock the door fast enough, she missed the call. Checking caller id, she recognized Lorenzo's number. The voicemail indicator came on and she pushed the button to listen. He had just heard from their mutual friend Kyle in Dallas. His wedding date was set for the first week in December.

The official invitations would be in the mail soon but he suggested booking the flight and hotel sooner rather than later. His fiancé had just discovered there was a convention of certified public accountants in the same hotel as the wedding. He ended by jokingly asking if she was up for yet another wedding.

Not in the mood to think happy thoughts that should always go along with weddings, Jennifer postponed calling him back until later that night. Despite trying to sound cheerful, Lorenzo sensed something was off. Changing his manner of voice from jovial to concerned, he asked what was wrong. She didn't mean to have a meltdown but was unable to say the words without her voice shaking and tears springing to her eyes again. She hadn't lost a patient in months and this time it really hit her hard. He listened sympathetically and tried say reassuring words of comfort. His heart ached for her as the agonizing pain in her voice was clearly evident.

Feeling exhausted from her emotional ordeal, Jennifer apologized for making him listen to her pathetic troubles. He assured her that it was no trouble and he was happy to be there for her anytime. Suddenly he asked her address. "Oh, great!" she thought. "Now he thinks he needs to send me a sympathy card or something." After giving him the information, Lorenzo did the strangest thing. He abruptly said he had to go but would contact her soon. Surprised by the change, she muttered a goodbye and hauled herself up off the sofa to get a much needed shower.

A couple of hours later her home phone rang with the tone indicating someone was buzzing her from the front entrance to her building. Alarmed, she asked who was there and was startled to hear Lorenzo's deep voice announcing himself. After hitting the button to unlock the door to the building, she ran to the bathroom and was dismayed at what she saw looking back at her in the mirror. Her eyes were puffy and her nose a bright shade of pink after all the crying she had done that day. "Oh no. I'm a total mess," she scolded herself. Splashing some cold water on her face didn't seem to help either. Too late. Lorenzo was already knocking on her door.

Taking a deep breath she opened the door. Without a word, Lorenzo reached out and drew her into an embrace. They moved inside the condo without breaking apart. As the door closed behind them, her tears started again. He held her as she sobbed. It wasn't until her body relaxed against his and her tears were spent that he gently pulled away just a little to look into her eyes. She saw his sympathy for what she was going through but she also saw something else. Almost as if it pained him to see her like this.

Realizing she must look a mess, Jennifer made to move away to get some tissues. Instead, Lorenzo tenderly stroked her cheek to wipe away a stray tear. His large hand cupped her face tenderly as he continued to gaze into her watery eyes. Not even realizing what she was doing, Jennifer leaned towards him and put her arms around his neck. Slowly, as if afraid to break away but also afraid to move closer, he tilted his head so they were eye to eye, nose to nose. Moments passed where Jennifer could only feel her heart thudding in her chest. Finally he closed the final distance and softly touched his lips to hers.

Tenderly at first and then with more urgency as long pent-up desire welled in them both, they kissed. His soft, sensual lips covering hers. As the kiss intensified his tongue parted her lips with a light stroke. The movement sent thrilling shivers through her body that left her hungry for more of him. Their tongues explored one another as if dancing to their own soft ballad. Deep inside her, Jennifer felt heat waves of passion surging throughout the body. From her very core to her limbs, long denied feelings bubbled up numbing her mind to anything else but the luscious feel of his body pressed against hers.

Lorenzo deftly guided them towards the oversized chair which was the first piece of furniture he could find. He settled her into the chair and knelt in front of her without breaking their connection. His hands caressed her face and neck as he deepened the kiss. Desperate to have him even closer her hands found the open collar on his shirt which she used to tug him closer to her. All thoughts had vacated her mind as soon as his lips had touched hers. There was nothing but sensation and the fire scorching through her veins.

Breathless, he pulled away to look into her blazing emerald eyes. There was a question in his eyes that remained unasked. Jennifer answered, without hesitation, as she pulled his head back towards hers. The intensity of their mutual need for each other was unable to be denied any longer. Had it always been there? Lorenzo gently scooped her up in his arms and moved them towards her bedroom.

Hours later, as the sun began to shine through her bedroom window, Jennifer stretched like a satiated cat as she ran her hand over Lorenzo's muscular sleeping form. The light streaming between the blinds only accentuated the perfection that was the man. Despite knowing him for years and seeing him in everything from a tuxedo to swim trunks, never would she have dared imagined him like this. Naked, in her bed, with his tousled hair covering his eyes as he continued to slumber. Jennifer reached up to move the hair away from his beautiful face so she could get a better look. Seeing him asleep it was hard to believe this angel was the same man that had taken her to such dizzying heights of ecstasy last night. She blushed at the memories.

Then realization struck. If he was here, who was with Raphael? How had she not thought of him before? She shook Lorenzo awake. He groggily sat up and reached for her as if to replay the events of last night, but she stopped him by the distraught look on her face. "Hey, I thought we got rid of that facial expression last night. What happened while I was asleep?" he asked.

She couldn't believe he didn't know. "Raphael. What about your son? Please tell me you didn't leave him alone just to come all this way to console me," she begged. With a huge sigh and laugh, he told her that the reason it had taken him so long to get here last night was because he packed up Raphael and sent him to a sleepover at a friend's house. Jennifer nearly collapsed back on the bed in relief. Of course he had taken care of his son first. Seeing her concern for the boy, Lorenzo smiled up at her and pulled her close. First he kissed her eyelids, then trailed light kisses down her face and neck before coming back to her mouth. They fell back on the bed together and spent the rest of the early morning enjoying each other.

A couple hours later, they had both showered and dressed. He needed to get back to coach his son's soccer game that afternoon. She had rounds to complete at the hospital and she was already late. As Lorenzo kissed her goodbye he asked her to come out to the game and spend time with him and Raphael for the weekend. Maybe she could even pack an overnight bag, he suggested. An offer like that was too good to refuse so she agreed to text him when she reached the Metro station closest to Warrenton. With a final longing kiss, they parted ways for the day. Both anticipating seeing each other again in just a few hours. Both exhilarated by their realized passion for each other and both nervous about where that left them as friends.

Jennifer found herself smiling like a silly lovesick girl as she made her rounds at the hospital. A couple nurses read the signs and were happy for the beautiful workaholic doctor. They commented, "It's about time that girl got a man!" Even the fretful parents of her patients picked up on her improved demeanor. This was a side to their child's doctor they had never witnessed. It was refreshing. The only person not happy about Jennifer's improved mood was Jacob. Although he had never officially made a move on her, he still thought of her as the one he would eventually captivate and marry. She had all the attributes of the perfect wife – gorgeous, highly intelligent, career-centric, and most importantly, she could charm the bigwigs in Washington out of their money for the hospital with just a bat of her eye lashes. Yes, Jennifer was his ideal candidate for the job of Mrs. Jacob Mallory. She, of course, was completely unaware of his plans.

As she finished with her files and put them back at the nurse's desk with specific instructions for each patient, Jacob approached her. As she turned to leave, she nearly bumped into him. "Sorry, Jacob. Didn't realize you were there," she apologized and made to go around him as she was anxious to get out to Warrenton for Raphael's game. He blocked her way and instead took her arm and led her to his office on the pretense of needing to consult about a patient. Reluctantly, Jennifer followed.

As they sat down in his office, he coolly commented on her changed behavior. Jennifer could tell he was not happy about something but was not in the mood to wait around to find out why. He continued, "Normally, I would be ecstatic seeing you so smiling and downright jovial with the staff and patients." His tone indicated he was not ecstatic at all. Quite the opposite. "However, it seems after you lost your patient just yesterday that perhaps you would become less distracted and refocus on saving the others instead of happily humming as you complete paperwork." His objective was clear – make her doubt herself and refocus the blame on the patient's death on her to guilt her into leaving behind whoever was diverting her attention from her work even for a second.

At first she was bewildered that he considered her to be unfocused on her patients and her work. After a few moments thought, she realized he could be right. Even she was astutely aware that ever since she had reconnected with Lorenzo, she found her mind drifting to him. Jennifer had convinced herself it was only when she was away from the hospital and not that often. After last night's events, maybe it had been more than that and she just hadn't realized it.

Observing the look of doubt cross her face, Jacob went in for the kill. "Perhaps you need something to fire your motivation for your research. There's a fundraiser tonight at Smithsonian. Why don't you come with me? You can redouble your efforts if more money is flowing in for research." Sadly defeated, she shook her yes and left the office. Jacob sat back in his chair with a smug smile.

Her new found pep vanished as she exited the hospital. "He was right," she chided herself, "I could've saved that suffering child if I had just spent more time at the hospital, more time researching the new protocol so it could've been used before it was too late.

This was all my fault. What was I thinking that I could have a personal life now? I've done without one for years. Obviously I don't need a man or love, and certainly not a family. My life's work is at a crucial stage. I can't allow myself to be diverted any longer. I owe it to the other children in that ward. Despite her heart and body screaming their need for Lorenzo, she resolved to end things with him before she lost the will to do so.

Tears rolled down her freckled face as she dialed Lorenzo's number. It went straight to voicemail so she left a short message saying there had been some complications at work and she would be unable to make Raphael's game. Unable to hold herself together when he called back just a few moments later, she turned off her phone and headed back home. The condo seemed so much lonelier without him. She thought, "Has it really only been a few hours since Lorenzo was here holding her, kissing her, making love to her?" It seemed like a lifetime ago now.

Without feeling much like going to a party, much less a charity event with Jacob, she dressed in a subdued gray chiffon number that fell off one shoulder. She may look dazzling but she didn't feel the part. Jennifer just went through the motions that evening. Smiling when talking with potential donors. Allowing Jacob to usher her around the room as his own personal property. She was even caught unawares when he introduced her to a high-ranking senator as his girlfriend. It jolted her out of her reverie like being struck by lightning. Unwilling to make a scene or embarrass him in front of the party guests, she continued to smile even when the senator made a remark to Jacob about not letting such a beauty get away. Jacob, of course, was in agreement with the suggestion.

Later that night, his car dropped Jennifer off at her condominium building. Jacob tried to convince her to invite him upstairs for nightcap and perhaps more. The entire ride back he had spent making allusions to how they made such a great "power couple". Not in the mood to deal with him and not wanting to risk her job at the hospital by giving him a piece of her mind, she bolted from the car without as much as a goodbye. "How could she have allowed him to manipulate her like that?" she wondered. It took his antics tonight to reveal the creep underneath. He wasn't worried about her neglecting her patients or research. He was only concerned about alienating her from everyone else so she would be vulnerable to him. How could she not have seen it before? Racking her brain for signs that she had missed, she recalled overhearing some nurses commenting about "poor sweet doctor" being preyed upon by "the big guy" and being completely oblivious. They had been talking about her, hadn't they? Honestly, Jennifer didn't know who she was more angry with...Jacob for pushing doubt into her mind that she was not a good doctor because she wasn't focused enough on her work and making her believe it was her fault patients died or herself for believing him. She had denied herself any life for years due to her own self-doubts. He had merely amplified that doubt and handicapped her emotionally so she wouldn't stray from her work, stray from his sight and control. Perhaps the best place to lay her anger was at her own feet for allowing it to happen.

She was so caught up in her inner rage that she didn't see the tall shadow come up behind her as she opened the front door to the building. It wasn't until she moved into the building and saw a muscular arm reach out to hold the door open that she turned around in fright. She was shocked to see Lorenzo standing in the doorway with an anguished look. What he was thinking she couldn't guess. They had made plans to be together that day and she had wimped out by leaving him a message with no explanation. Now here she was dolled up from her night on the town with her boss. They stood in the vacant foyer staring at each other in the dark for several moments before Lorenzo turned to leave without saying a word. Desperate to explain, she reached for him but he flung her arm back.

As he brusquely walked out the door, a pouring rain had just started. Jennifer rushed out to stop him, but he continued briskly walking to wherever he had parked his SUV. Unable to keep up in her 2 inch heels, she stopped only long enough to pull them from her feet. The shoes were left there as she raced after him. Even though she was a fast runner and had placed in the last Marine Corps marathon, Jennifer found it difficult to keep up. As he neared his car, she dashed across the street unaware of an approaching taxi. The last thing she saw was Lorenzo's look of horror as he turned to see the collision. Then everything went dark.

Jennifer awoke to a throbbing in her head and the incessant beeping of heart rate monitor. Placing her hand to her head and feeling the large lump, she moaned in pain. The sound awakened the sleeping giant beside her bed. Despite everything, Lorenzo had stayed with her. Her mind was still too fuzzy from the accident that she couldn't begin to understand why after she had ditched him and his son last night. Perhaps he could forgive her not showing up for him, but letting Raphael down – she doubted anyone could forgive that. She certainly didn't forgive herself.

Lorenzo took her hand and asked how she felt. Instead of saying the expected response like "fine" or "horrible" or any derivative of the two, she simply said "stupid". Thinking she meant stupid for running out into the street in front an oncoming car, he nodded agreement. "Haven't you heard of looking both ways before you cross the road?" he challenged.

Her head still groggy and her thoughts jumbled, she tried to explain that it wasn't being hit by the car that was stupid. It was how she had convinced herself that she was a horrible person for wanting a life, wanting him and his son in her life instead of spending every waking moment under Jacob's thumb at the hospital.

She tried explaining how he had manipulated her into doubting her dedication to her patients and guilted her into going to a hospital fundraiser instead of where she belonged at Raphael's game. It was stupid to believe she couldn't be a good doctor if she allowed herself to have anything or anyone else in her life. It was stupid not to realize that she wanted, that she needed love too. And it was stupid of her not to realize all this time that she needed and loved him.

By the time she finished speaking, they were both in tears. The nurse came in to check on her patient to find the doctor and her hot looking companion holding each other as if for dear life. She recognized the signs, so she quickly and quietly left in order to disturb the lovebirds.

As she was signing her release papers, Jacob stopped by her room. Lorenzo recognized him as the gentleman that had dropped Jennifer off the night before. He certainly didn't like the way the man was looking at her. By the expression on her face, Jennifer wasn't happy to see him but she motioned for Lorenzo to wait outside.

Jacob tried apologizing for not walking her in, as if that would have prevented the accident. Unable to contain her emotions any longer she let into him for all the years he had spent parading her around like an ornament at charity events. All the while belittling her work and making her doubt her own dedication and ability to saving children's lives. It had all been for his benefit.

With her by his side he could raise money supposedly for her research, but she never saw a dime of that money. She was always scrapping by with used equipment and no personnel. Despite the odds, she still made significant progress. Exhausted from her long overdue rant against him, she verbally gave him her notice of resignation. She would take her research and skills to another hospital.

After he left, Lorenzo returned awestruck by what he had heard through the thin glass doors. Apparently, the entire floor had heard her accusations as there was applause from the nurse's station as Jacob stormed off to his office. With a look of admiration, he shook his head. "Well, does this mean you have some time to hang out with a young man who is desperately waiting to hear the news that you are okay, and with his old man?"

"After all this, do you really still want me around? It's not like we can just go back to the other night and pretend none of this happened," she replied.

"Yes, WE," he emphasized, "want you around. And not just for a soccer game. Not just as an overnight guest. Not as just a convenient date for weddings." Holding her bruised face in his hands, he looked into her eyes and confessed, "I want you, need you in my life. Ever since college, I've been in mad love with you but knew you didn't feel the same. For years I hid behind the status of friend.

Too afraid to speak up even when you took off for medical school." He continued as she stared at him in disbelief, "Seeing you again brought all those feelings rushing back but you still showed no signs of wanting anything other than a platonic friendship. You were only focused on your work. I understand your need to help save lives. I understand your desire to find the cure so other children don't have to suffer like your friend Hannah. I understand all that and love you for all that and more. You've just been too blind to see it," he confessed.

Whoa! Jennifer didn't trust her ears on that last part. "Did he just say 'love'?" she questioned herself. With new tears rolling down her face, she nearly punched him. "Love? You've been in love with me and never said a word? Are you sure you don't want to take that back? Better do it quickly before I hold you to that." In reply, he pulled her close. The kiss that followed was soft, yet deep and all-consuming.

The pounding in her head was no more. The only pounding she felt was her own heart. She pulled back for just a moment to ask, "And how does Raphael feel about all this?"

A few months later in Dallas, Lorenzo and Raphael escorted Jennifer into the wedding ceremony for Kyle and his bride. Ever since that day in the hospital they had been together. She had been true to her word and resigned from Georgetown University Hospital. After taking some much needed and deserved time off, she had just accepted a job offer at a private research facility and hospital being built on the outskirts of the DC metropolitan area as their director of pediatric cancer research. The condo in Georgetown sold quickly, as the district never suffered from the housing market bust like the rest of the country. Presently, she was renting a townhouse in Warrenton so she could be close to "her boys".

Her relationship with Raphael had bloomed quickly. They were completely attached to each other. Even the blonde teacher's assistant that had been so rude to her at the other wedding admitted that Jennifer was devoted and loving to the boy. The soccer team adopted her as the team "mom" as she always brought them healthy snacks and tended to their bumps and bruises.

There had been one instance where Raphael had been hit in the head with the ball so hard that he was knocked out for a few moments. Jennifer hadn't realized until then just how much she had grown to love him as she begged and pleaded with God for Raphael to wake up and be okay. He was, of course, but she could no longer deny she wanted to be a mother to him.

As for her relationship with Lorenzo...Jennifer wanted to kick herself every day for being blind to his feeling for her for so long, and blind to her feelings for him. He didn't allow her to wallow in regret though. The time was much better spent making up for lost time, which happen to include making lots and lots of love. Despite their need to be together, she insisted on keeping her own apartment. She didn't want Raphael to be upset having another woman sleeping his dad's bed. If they have bothered to ask, Raphael would have gladly told them otherwise.

Jennifer could not believe how blessed she was having Lorenzo and Raphael in her life. As she sat in the church pew flanked on both sides by the men she loved and listening to the words being said by the priest about love and family, she finally realized just how important those things were. Nearly missing her opportunity for true love gave her a greater appreciation for the words being spoken for the bride and groom. Lorenzo wasn't just her wedding date. He wasn't just her boyfriend. He and his sweet son were her life.

After the lovely ceremony, the wedding party adjourned to the large, heated tent erected on the local minor league baseball field. Turns out Kyle's company did considerable business with the team's owner who had loaned them the location for the reception. After dinner and dancing, Raphael was showing signed of fatigue so they decided to return to their hotel. Lorenzo seemed reluctant to leave and then excused himself for a moment. Confused, she stayed with Raphael as they waited for their coats.

A few moments later the strands of Frank Sinatra's "The Way You Look Tonight" began to play. Lorenzo returned and without a word ushered Jennifer out onto the dance floor for one final dance. Raphael stood just to the side of the dance floor watching them intently. As she leaned her head against his chest and listened to his heart thumping she became concerned it was beating so quickly.

Towards the end of the song, Lorenzo dropped to one knee and gazed up at her with such a mixed expression of fear and longing. She didn't immediately notice the small box he had pulled out of his suit jacket. Confused, she stared in disbelief as the music faded away and Lorenzo uttered the words he had been waiting years to say to her. "Jennifer, my love, you are my heart and soul. I can no longer live without you. I want, I need you as my wife and my partner in life. Raphael wants and needs you as his mother." With that the boy ran over to the couple looking up at her with the most beautiful expectant expression. Lorenzo continued, "Jennifer, will you marry me?"

There it was. The question she hadn't realized she had wanted to hear so badly. Almost unable to speak, she looked into Raphael's face and then Lorenzo's and she knew that she was home. With happy tears streaming down her face, "Yes," she whispered, "yes."

******

For Keeps

Scott Mitchell and Tiffany Reynolds have been best friends since grade school. Although Scott knew that he and Tiffany would never end up being a "couple," he always hoped that they would end up together one day. He was disheartened when Tiffany chose to move three thousand miles away to New York City to pursue a career in advertising. When Tiffany graduated two years earlier, Scott hoped she would have moved back home to the small California town in which they both grew up in.

However, that didn't happen, and because of this, Scott was only able to see Tiffany when she returned home during the holidays. This always put him in a sad mood because he wasn't able to see his best friend as much as he would have like to. While he had lots of guy friends, Scott never felt close enough to any of them to share his inner feelings in the same way he was able to do with Tiffany.

As the years dragged on, Scott slowly began realizing that it wasn't their best friend status that left him wanting Tiffany closer, it was the fact that he had true feelings for her and he never felt at ease to tell her.

That was all going to change and soon. He flipped open his cellphone and replayed her message:

"Hey, Scott. It's your BFF. I just wanted to let you know that I am heading back in town and I have some news for you...actually two pieces of news for you. I'm sorry that I missed you, but I will call you as soon as the plane touches down. Love you Scott. Talk to you soon!"

He disconnected the call. He didn't know why he saved it, but he just felt compelled to. That call came in twelve hours, four minutes, and thirty-three seconds ago. He couldn't wait to have her call back. "I am such a loser," he moaned to himself. "Here I am pining away for a girl that I wanted nothing to do with when we were ten years old. If I would have known then, what I know now." He said, shaking his head. He grabbed a change of clothes and went into the bathroom. He started the shower and got undressed.

As the water washed over him, he could hear the sound of his cell phone. He quickly stepped out of the shower, not caring that the water was still running. He wrapped a towel around his body and headed back into his bedroom, reaching the phone before it hung up. "Hello?"

"Scott?"

His heart skipped a beat, hearing her voice. "Tiff? I wasn't expecting your call so soon."

"Did I wake you?" She asked.

"No," he replied, sinking down on the bed. "I was just taking a shower." He cursed himself for being so vocal, when he heard the hesitation. "It's good to hear your voice, Tiff."

She chuckled. He loved the sound of her laughing. "You hear my voice all the time. I call you more than I call my mother."

"You know what I mean. It's great to hear your voice, knowing that you're back in California." He replied, crossing his fingers. "You are in California, right?"

"Yes, I am. The plane touched down about ten minutes ago. I told you that I would call you right away."

Scott smiled to himself. It made him feel good that he was the first call she made. "Do you need a ride somewhere? I could come get you and be there in less than twenty minutes." He looked down at his wet body and shrugged. He would take the fastest shower anyone has ever taken if he had to.

"That's sweet, Scott, but I'm going to get a rental. Thanks for the offer though."

"Sure, no problem," he states, a little disappointed.

The awkward silence builds and he fights the urge to talk too much, but he can sense something is on her mind. "So, what's new?" He asks, hoping it didn't come across as a strange question.

"A lot," she confesses. "In fact, I was hoping that maybe we could talk this evening for supper. If you're not busy."

He thought about his busy work schedule, but he could move some things around. "Tonight would be perfect."

"Great! I will plan on meeting at our place about 6:30."

He smiled, knowing that she meant *Uncle Tony's Pizzeria.* "I will see you then." He replied, disconnecting. He went back to his shower, feeling excited about the evening. He was ready to tell her the truth and hope for the best, or at least hope that she wouldn't choose to discontinue their friendship.

***

Tiffany wrung her hands together. She could feel her heart thumping in her chest and she didn't know why she was so nervous. She glanced around the restaurant and saw that he was still not there. He was her best friend and the fact that she felt like she was getting ready to see a stranger was weird. They didn't see each other often, but when they did it was like they had never been apart.

She looked up and saw him rushing into the restaurant. She took a deep breath and stood up. He hurried to her. "I am so sorry for being late." He kissed her cheek, "It was a busy day at work."

"No problem. I wasn't worried. I knew you would show." She smiled at him. He looked at her and grinned. For a moment she was reminded how she grew up having the biggest crush on him and he never seemed to notice. She cleared her throat, "I figured we didn't need to look in the menu."

He smiled, "You would be correct." He looked at her, "You're looking good, Tiff."

She blushed, "Thanks. You don't look half bad yourself." Their easy banter would pick up. It always did. The waitress walked over and they ordered their usual Pineapple and Pepperoni pizza, something only the two of them would enjoy. She then turned back to him. "So, how have you been? Any new girlfriends I should know about?" She took a drink of her soda and he laughed.

"Not quite. You know me...I'm involved with my job. Isn't that enough?"

She thought about that. It was true that he did seem to be a workaholic, but he always found time to make for her. "I have a feeling when you find that someone special then that will all change."

He smiled, "Think so, huh?"

She nodded, confidently. "I actually have some things that I want to discuss with you."

"Hm..." he replied. "I thought this impromptu supper was because you missed me."

She shrugged, "Well, that's true too."

"Okay, I feel a little bit better," he spoke with a laugh. "I actually have some things that I want to discuss with you too."

"You do?" She asked, surprised.

"I do, but I thought maybe we could wait a little bit before I delve into that. So, feel free to begin."

She waited for a moment, trying to figure out how she wanted to proceed. She had been rehearsing the way she was going to tell him for several weeks now, but it all seemed to go out of her mind. "It can wait. How's your family been?"

He raised his eyebrows. "That's changing the subject, but they have been doing really well. Sid just started at the University and Bryce is a senior this year."

"Wow. That's hard to believe. I remember when they were just—"

"Pests...bothering us relentlessly?"

She laughed, "I was going to say that I remember when they weren't even in school yet. I feel old."

"Tell me about it," he replied, chuckling.

The waitress came with their food and they fell into an easy silence as they started to eat. "I really am excited that you're here."

She smiled, "Me too." She took another bite and figured she would wait until they were done eating, before bringing up the reason she was in town. "Has work been going okay?" She asked, stopping to take a drink.

"Busy as ever, but loving every minute of it. I should ask you how your jobs going? After all, working at a big time ad agency must have some perks."

She nodded, but barely made eye contact. "It's been great, but I actually quit there two weeks ago."

His jaw dropped, "Must not be that great. Why did you do that?"

She shrugged, "Had my reasons."

He put down his slice of pizza. "We have known each other for almost twenty years and have been best friends for fourteen of those years. You aren't going to get away with that. What happened?"

She groaned, taking her last bite of pizza. "I'm moving back to California."

"What? Are you serious? When were you going to tell me that?"

"Tonight," she replied nonchalantly. "I was waiting for the perfect moment. Are you surprised?"

"Um...yeah, I'm surprised." A smile is on his face, but then he starts to frown. "May I ask why? I mean you seemed so happy when you made the decision to stay there. What changed?"

She knew that it was the moment she had been practicing for. "Well...my fiancé is getting transferred." That wasn't exactly how she envisioned telling him, but it got the point across.

He stared at her and then shook his head, "I'm sorry, I thought you just said that your fiancé is getting transferred."

"That's exactly what I said. Surprise...I'm getting married."

She couldn't read his mind to see how he felt about the news. She knew that he wasn't expecting it, when she had only been dating Erick for a month. She hadn't even told her family or Scott that she was seeing someone. "When did this happen?" He asked.

"He proposed a couple days ago, but he asked me to move to California with him two weeks ago."

"I'm sorry that I am finding this a little hard to believe. I mean, up until about five seconds ago I didn't even know you were dating anyone. Now, to hear that you are moving to California with your fiancé? It's a lot to take in."

"I know," she replied quietly. "I didn't plan it. One day I was meeting him, the next day he was telling me that he loved me, then he was saying that he was getting transferred to California, and asking me to go with him. It just all happened so quickly, but I do love him."

"You do?" He replied softly.

She didn't need time to consider it. She knew that in her heart she felt love for him. "He gets me in ways that not too many people do." She looked down at her empty plate, "Similar to ways that you get me."

He nodded, taking another bite of his pizza. "Wow...I am just in shock."

She knew he would be, because outside of the occasional dating she never really was too involved with boys. She never seemed to have time for them, when she was too preoccupied with other things going on in her life. "Are you happy for me?" She asked, carefully considering the question.

He slowly nodded, but then added a smile. "Of course I'm happy for you. It's just going to take some time to get used to." He hesitated, looking down at the table, "When am I going to meet him?"

"He'll be in town in a few days." She said. "I wanted to prepare my family...and you, before you met him." She replied, but part of her still wondered why she was worried about what they would thing...especially Scott. She couldn't explain it, but she was most worried how Scott would react to him.

***

Scott had to process the news. The minute Tiffany told him she was getting married, he found himself sick. They went on with their meal, like nothing was happening inside of him, but he was finding it difficult to concentrate. He wanted to be happy for her, but the thought of losing her to another guy was too much to bear.

"I am so relieved that you took the news this way." She was saying.

"Oh...why's that?" He asked, taking a drink.

She shrugs, "I don't know. I guess you're opinion matters to me." It was a simple response, but he questioned if that was all. "It was actually more difficult telling you, than it will be to tell my parents."

Scott slowly nodded and then glanced down at her finger. He didn't even want to bother asking why she wasn't wearing the ring. He figured she did that so that she could tell people, without having them see the ring first. "Maybe it's because I was your first husband." He frowned, "Come to think of it...did we ever officially get divorced? You might want to check into that, before you say you'll marry this guy."

Her eyes got big, but then she smiled and started to laugh. "The playground marriage, who could forget that?" She shrugged, "I'm pretty sure the marriage was dissolved the day that you carried Sissy Baker's books to her class in ninth grade." She shook her head and acted like she was crying, "It broke my heart."

He smiled, "She was a tough girl. She threatened to beat me up if I didn't carry her books." He winked at her and she laughed. "I was only trying to save my life." He thought on what he wanted to say next and his mind drifted back to his dream that he woke up to. "I have actually been thinking about that marriage." He admitted.

She smirked, "You have?"

He nodded, "Yep and it occurred to me that I don't even remember how it came about." He shrugged, "I guess it really doesn't matter, but it's something that I have wondered."

"You mean...you don't remember the undying love you had for me?" She took a piece of her pizza and shook her head, "I am hurt." She took a bite and he could see her smiling.

"I have to admit, I did have a thing for girls in pigtails." He replied, laughing.

She snickered and nodded, "I figured." She looked down at her plate and he could see that she was thinking about that day. "Don't you remember? You wanted to play on the monkey bars and I told you that I would only let you do that if we got married." She smiled, "I was pretty tough back then."

He thought about that and then the realization snuck in. He laughed, "That's right. The monkey bars get me all the time." He turned quiet and then looked at her, "You know, that was really the start of our friendship."

She raised her eyebrows and then nodded. "We've been close ever since."

He could see that there was something on her mind and he decided to try to find out what was going on. "I can tell something's bothering you."

"This won't change anything, Scott. We'll still be friends."

The way she said that, caused a knot in his chest. "I know we will. Just not best friends, because that will be reserved for your husband. I get that." He told her everything that he needed to tell her, but in his mind he was fumbling with the words. He was going to have a hard time getting over this.

***

Tiffany laid in bed, her eyes were focused on a picture of Scott and her that they had taken in a mall photo booth. She wanted to believe that everything was going to be alright when it came to their friendship, but her head was telling her that nothing was going to ever be the same. Things at her parent's house went fine. They were happy for them and no doubts were left behind.

She heard her cellphone ringing and she reached it from the bed. She glanced at the caller ID and saw that it was Erick. She answered the call. "Hello?"

"Hey, babe." He said. "How was your first day back?"

She looked at the picture and then placed it on the hotel nightstand. "It went well." She smiled to herself, "When does your plane arrive?"

"Well, that's one of the reasons I was calling." He said. His voice sounded apologetic.

"Yes?" She asked.

"I just found out that the transfer isn't going to be finalized for two more weeks."

The phone nearly fell from her hands. "Are you serious?"

"I'm sorry Babe, but I have to stay here until that becomes definite."

She couldn't believe this was happening. "I came here now, because I thought that you would be following shortly behind." She looked around her hotel room, "What should I do here while I wait for you to arrive?"

"Well...maybe you could start looking for a house for us to live in. Plus, you still have to find a job."

She nodded slowly, "Fine," she said, knowing that the disappointment was there.

"Babe, don't be like that." He says. His voice held concern, but she wasn't at the point of worrying about that. "We will be together soon and it will be like we were never apart."

"I know," she sadly replied. "I will see what I can do without you here."

"I love you," he replied.

She let out a breath, "I love you, too. Goodbye." She hung up the phone and turned to the picture of Scott. She dialed up his number, hoping it wasn't too late. He answered quickly, showing that it wasn't a problem. "Hey, Scott."

"Hello...miss me already?"

She smiled to herself, "Not quite."

"Ouch, I'm hurt," he teased.

She rolled her eyes, "I was just calling to see what you were doing this weekend."

There was a hesitation on his end and she wondered if maybe she was too quick to jump to the conclusion that he wouldn't be busy. "Well, I..." he started, but she quickly broke in.

"I am sure you are busy. I didn't mean to be insensitive. You have a life. We can get together later."

"Tiffany, are you through?" He asked. She closed her mouth and didn't say anything else. "I have a lunch meeting with a client, but after that I have no plans. Did you want me to meet your fiancé? I hope," he replied, laughing.

"Well, not exactly. It turns out that he won't be coming back for a couple more weeks." She paused, "long story. I just thought that maybe we could go to some of the old places we used to go."

"Well, I think that that would be a fabulous idea." He replied. "I could pick you up at the hotel about two o'clock. If that works for you?"

"That would be great," she agreed. "See you in a few days. Goodnight."

"Goodnight," he said, as they disconnected the call. She put the phone back on the nightstand. She knew that beginning the following week she would need to start looking for that perfect job. She laid back in bed and closed her eyes. She would have plenty of things to do to keep herself busy, until Erick was arriving in California.

***

Scott picked her up at two o'clock sharp. He didn't want to question why her fiancé wasn't going to be there until later. He didn't really care. He was happy to step in and show her a good time. He walked up to her hotel room door and knocked. She opened up the door instantly. Her smile always caught him off guard. She left the hotel room and glanced up at me. "Thank you for wanting to get together."

"Of course." They fell into an easy stride with one another.

"How did your meeting go today?" She asked.

He was always surprised with how much she seemed interested in what he was doing. "It went well. I signed him on with a contract." They left the hotel and walked to his car. He stood at the passenger side, opening the door for her.

"Thank you!" She replied, getting into his car. He hurried around to the other side. "Where are we going first?" She asked.

"I have my preferences, but I suppose it can be your choice." He said, hoping she would choose their favorite ice cream shop.

"You want dessert?" She asked.

He laughed, "You read my mind." He put the vehicle into motion and they headed toward their destination. "So, you were rather vague on the phone. Why isn't your fiancé coming to California yet?"

She looked out the window, like she didn't want to make eye contact. "His work put a delay on his transfer." She shrugged, turning to face him. "I guess that it gives me time to sort out of my life here. I have to find a job and I can start looking for houses."

"Alone?" He asked, trying not to butt in.

She nodded, "It might not be the best scenario, but I can always send him pics of what I find and get his opinion. Right?"

He could tell that she was trying to be stronger about it than she was letting on, but he couldn't make her feel worse. "Of course."

She smiled, turning back and glancing out the window. He felt for her and couldn't believe how her fiancé would be willing to wait this long to meet up with her. He had a hard time being that far away from her and they weren't even dating. He pulled into the ice cream shop and her demeanor instantly changed. She seemed happy. "This is exactly what I need. Marla's famous double scoop fudge—"

"Peanut butter ice cream sundae," he finished for her.

She nodded, "I can taste it already." They got out of the car and headed into the small building. The minute they were seated, the teenaged girl approached them.

"Hello, my name is Noelle. Would you like a menu?"

They both shook their heads, "That won't be necessary," Tiffany responded, ordering the two desserts. "Thank you!" She said, watching the girl walk away. "Remember when I worked here?" She asked, turning back to Scott. "The outfits haven't changed."

He laughed, "This place was hopping on Friday nights after football games, but you seemed to love it."

She nodded, "I did." As her words came out, he spotted Marla heading their way. Tiffany looked up and jumped to her feet. "Marla..." she pulled her into a hug. "I have missed you." When she parted, it looked like she had tears in her eyes.

"We have missed you too, When I saw the order, I just knew that it would be my two favorite customers." Marla spoke with a smile. She turned to Scott and nodded. "Scott, good to see you too."

"Thank you Marla...likewise."

"So, what brings you back to California?" Marla asked, focusing back on Tiffany.

"Well, I am moving back to town."

"Her fiancé will be joining her shortly," Scott said. When Tiffany looked at him, he wasn't sure if it was anger or shock that he said anything. He was leaning more toward anger.

"Fiancé?" Marla asked, looking down and noticing the ring on her left hand. Her jaw dropped. "Holy cow...what does he do for a living?"

"He's a lawyer and he is transferring the branch in town." She held out her hand and Scott caught himself looking at it again. Each time he thought about the fact that she was getting married, he cringed. He looked up, forcing himself not to look at her engagement ring. There was a smile on her face, but there was also sadness in her eyes. He could feel it.

"Well, congratulations." Marla turned back to me and smiled, "I must admit, I always thought maybe the two of you would end up together." She laughed, "Apparently, I am not destined to be a psychic." She grinned, "Glad to have you home."

She walked away and Tiffany took her seat. Her face was red and I watched her for a second, before clearing my throat and trying to lighten the mood. "It must be that darn wedding when we were ten. It has people all confused."

She looked up and laughed, "Is that it?"

He shrugged, "Makes perfect sense." He looked up and saw the ice cream heading to their table. "Perfect timing." The girl put the ice creams down. "Thank you," he said, handing Tiffany a spoon. "Dig in."

They each took a bite as Tiffany sighed. "Heavenly."

He took a bite and nodded in agreement. This was something that would take away all worries and doubts and nothing was going to change that.

***

Tiffany waited by the car, as Scott disappeared. He gave no explanation, but said he had a surprise for her. They had just finished at the ice cream shop and it definitely took her mind off of the fact that Scott wasn't going to be there.

She saw Scott heading back to the car. He was on the phone as he approached her. "We'll be there. Thank you Veronica." He disconnected the call, "Get in."

"Who was on the phone?" She asked, inquisitively.

"We are going to pick you out the perfect home." He replied with a smile. "I'll explain on the way." Tiffany wasn't sure about that, but got in anyway. He began to explain immediately. "Veronica Baylor is one of my clients and one of the top notch realtors in the area. I called her and asked her to put together a list of houses and we're going to meet her at one of them."

Her jaw dropped, "We're what?"

He glanced at her, "You heard me."

"Yeah, I heard you, but I don't feel like this is such a great idea. I mean...this is something that I am supposed to be doing with my future husband." She shrugged, "Seems strange."

He shook his head, "It's not strange. He isn't here and I am. It's better than going out alone. Besides, maybe I can help you get the perfect price." He turned back to the road. She was still apprehensive, but decided to go with it. He continued driving, until he turned onto a secluded street. He pulled up in front of a house that had a sale sign in front of it.

She looked at the house and imagined living there. It was fairly good size, but she would have to check the inside out. She got out of the car and they headed up to the door. From the car in the driveway, she knew that the realtor was already there.

He opened the door and called out, "Veronica?"

A tall woman came out of a room, wearing a smile. "Hello," she held out her hand and Tiffany shook it.

"Hello," Tiffany spoke. She was looking around the entrance of the house.

"Thank you for meeting us on such short notice," Scott was saying.

"Not a problem. Let me give you both the guided tour."

They followed her, through another room where she introduced the living room. It was a nice size room and Tiffany could picture the type of furniture they would get and where it would go. "This is a nice room," Scott was saying and she nodded.

"I'll show you the kitchen." As she led the way, she looked back at them. "When are you both getting married?" She asked.

"Um..." she glanced at Scott, looking for some help to explain it to her, but he was just smiling. "We're not." She finally spoke. The realtor looked away and she playfully hit him. He laughed.

"Tiffany is getting married. We're just friends."

"Oh..." Veronica said, seeming unfazed. "This is a nice kitchen. Do you like to cook?"

She opened her mouth to speak, but Scott was speaking instead. "She makes great peanut butter and jelly sandwiches." He replied. She glared at him and she could see that he was having a wonderful time on her behalf.

Veronica glanced back at her and Tiffany snickered, "I do alright in the kitchen." She turned and snared in his direction. "You are dead," she whispered.

He raised his eyebrows, but brushed past her as they entered the kitchen. "The best part of the house is the majority of appliances are staying."

"Why is the seller selling?" She asked, glancing at the nicely decorated room.

"She is getting older and her daughter lives out of town, so she decided to move closer to her daughter. She doesn't want a lot of her stuff."

"This is a nice kitchen," Tiffany mumbled, looking at the appliances. They each seemed fairly new. The tiled floor was also something that she liked.

"We can go upstairs where you will see the two bedrooms and a bathroom." They followed her out of the kitchen. When they reached the staircase, she pointed to another door. "There is a half bath right there." She led the way up the stairs and they reached the floor. She opened the door and they entered the room. "This is the master bedroom. It has a bathroom attached." She looked all over the bedroom. It was bigger than her New York bedroom, at least by three times.

"This is nice," she replied, opening up closets and stepping inside. In the bathroom, she could see the sink was completely made of ceramic and also looked brand new.

"Wow..." Scott mumbled, stepping in behind her.

She looked at him and nodded, "Nice, huh?" She whispered.

He nodded, "Definitely nicer than my apartment."

She smiled, as they stepped out of the bathroom. They exited the bedroom and looked at the other two. They were about the same, just smaller. "This is nice. Really it is," she started. They headed down the stairs and Veronica turned to her when they reached the foyer. "I am almost too afraid to ask the asking price."

Veronica held up her finger and disappeared back into the kitchen. "This is nice, but it's going to be way too expensive," she whispered to Scott.

Veronica came back into the foyer and looked over the paper. "You are looking at $115,000."

Tiffany gasped, figuring that it would be something like that. She opened her mouth, but again Scott was interrupting. "I'm sure that is just the asking price."

Veronica nodded, "I am sure that the owner would negotiate."

Tiffany tried to smile, "I appreciate the offer, but in order for us to be able to afford it...we would have to agree to way less than that. I am sure that she won't agree to negotiate that much. Thank you, but we'll have to keep looking." She headed out of the house, not wanting to think about it for another minute.

Scott joined her and they got into the car. "Don't you want to at least try?"

She thought about that, but then shook her head. "We have only looked at one house. I am sure there will be much more to look at. Thank you!" He turned from her and they waited until Veronica's car pulled out of the driveway and they followed her. She had no doubt that there would be plenty of houses that they could look into.

***

Scott dropped Tiffany back off at her hotel. He had one of the best times he could have even imagined just looking at houses with her. It felt like they were a couple that were getting ready to get married. He still didn't know how Erick could stand being away from her.

He got back home and threw his wallet and keys on the coffee table and crashed on the couch. He didn't know how he would pull it off, but he knew that he wouldn't feel right if he didn't try to win her heart. He couldn't give up without a fight.

He got off the couch and thought about ways to a woman's heart. He grabbed a notebook from the kitchen drawer and took a seat at the table. He began writing her a letter:

Dearest Tiffany:

I have tried numerous times to tell you what's in my heart, yet the words always fail me or you are with someone else. While this might not be the most opportune time, I feel that I have to be honest with you and myself. Since the first day I laid eyes on you, I knew that you were something special. It was after our fake marriage at the age of 10, that I began to realize that there was more to you.

You are beautiful inside and out and I have been blessed to call you my best friend, but over the years I have struggled with what's right and wrong. I have wanted to be happy for you and I am, to an extent. I have watched you pursue your dreams and I couldn't be more proud of that. I stood back and didn't say a word, when you chose to stay in New York City, even though my heart was being ripped from my chest. I hear news that you are getting married and I am left wondering how I could be so stupid.

I am asking you not to walk down that aisle, because what you need is and has always been right before your eyes. I love you, Tiffany and nothing is going to stop me from saying that. I have been too scared to admit it, but I am running out of time and this is my last hope. Please, give us a chance. You are everything I could ever want and I have to tell you that. I will remain by your side no matter what happens, but I am hoping that you can find it in your heart to say that you love me too.

Love,

Scott

He looks at the letter and almost crumples it up, but he can't. He spoke from the heart and that's all he could do. He did know that he couldn't give her the letter so soon. He would focus on other ways to get through to her and use the letter has a final piece. He closed the notebook up and left the kitchen. He needed to take a cold shower and try to put her out of his mind. It wouldn't be easy, but it was what needed to be done.

***

Tiffany yawned as she filled out her third application online. She hoped that one of the employers called her. She was just about to hit submit, when she heard a knock on her hotel room door. She quickly hit submit and then went to the door. She peered outside to find a man holding a bouquet of flowers at her door. She opened the door and smiled. "Hello."

"Hello. Are you Tiffany Reynolds?"

"Yes," she replied, staring at the bouquet of pink roses. They were her favorite color of roses.

He handed the flowers to her. "Enjoy!" He smiled, turning and walking away from her.

She looked down at the flowers and carried them back into the room. She placed them on the table and leafed through the bouquet, until she found the car. She removed it and read what it said:

Tiffany –
You are more beautiful now than the first day I saw you.
I hope these brighten your day.

She flipped the card over. It wasn't signed. "They have to be from Erick," she assured herself. She smelled the bouquet and smiled. "They sure are gorgeous," she mumbled, placing them on the table to brighten up the room. She heard her cellphone ringing and looked down to see that Scott was calling her. "Hey, Scott."

"Hey...what are you doing?"

She looked back at her computer and groaned, then looked at the flowers. "Staring at the most beautiful bouquet of roses. Erick knew the pick me up I needed." There was silence on the other end that she thought she had gotten disconnected. "Are you there?"

"Uh yeah...I'm here."

"So...what's up?" She asked, getting back to the reason he called.

"I thought maybe we could go out for lunch. I have some extra time, before having a meeting this afternoon."

"Sure, that would be great."

"Okay, meet you at my work at noon?"

"I'll be there," she replied. "See ya then," she hung up the call and looked back at the roses. She dialed up Erick's number. It went straight to his voicemail. She waited for the beep and then spoke, "Hey, babe...I just wanted to call you and tell you how much I love you and I miss you. I'm sure you're busy getting things finished up for work, but I can't wait to talk to you. Goodbye." She hung up the call. She wanted to hear his voice and thank him for the beautiful flowers, but it could wait. She walked back to the computer and closed it up. She would give it some time before applying for any more positions. She needed to get ready for lunch.

***

Scott couldn't concentrate. He should have known that she would assume the roses were from Erick. He groaned in frustration, tossing his pen. "What did this pen do to you?" He looked up to see Heather, his receptionist, standing in the door.

"Oh...thanks." He said, taking the pen from her. He hesitated, before looking up at her. "You're a woman."

"Thanks for the brilliant deduction," she replied with a laugh.

He smiled, "I just meant, out of curiosity what do women like to receive as gifts?"

"Flowers," she stated, with conviction.

"Been there...done that," he replied. "What else?"

She seemed to ponder on that. "Well, you can't go wrong with candy...chocolate especially." He had thought about that, but he was trying to get away from the usual gifts. He chose flowers, because he knew how much she loved pink roses. "Jewelry is always a plus." She replied, smiling. "I guess that most women really just go for something that comes from the heart." She shrugged, "Doesn't have to take a lot of thought, but it needs to be real."

He nodded, trying to think about that. Some ideas entered his mind and he thought that he would have to try them out. "Thank you. Now, did you need something?"

"I was going to let you know that I was going out for lunch. Do you need anything?"

"Nope, I will be heading out soon. Enjoy."

She smiled. She turned around, nearly running into Tiffany. "Hey, Heather." They hugged one another, but when they parted Heather turned back to me. A look of recognition in her eyes. I tried to ignore her, turning to Tiffany.

"Tiffany, I hear that congratulations is in order." She stuck her hand out, showing Heather. I had to roll my eyes, because I was getting tired of dwelling on it. "That is a beauty." She glanced back at Scott, "It's a beauty, isn't it Scott?"

Scott nodded, "It sure is." He stood up and walked to the door. "Are you ready to go?"

"I better get going," Heather said.

"Goodbye, Heather." He called, as she left the office. "Where do you want to go?"

She shook her head, "I don't care."

They headed to the door and left the building. As they walked down the street to the corner restaurant, she began talking about the flowers. He wanted to ask if she was trying to make him jealous, but decided against it. He opened the door for her and she entered. "How did he sign it?" He asked.

She turned to him, "That's kind of private, don't you think?"

"Oh excuse me," he replied, sarcastically. He walked up to the podium and the hostess had them follow her. When they sat down, he looked at the menu. "If you have some cute name for each other and you don't want to tell me how he signed it, then more power to you." He looked through the menu, hoping she would see that he wasn't bothered by her words; even though he was.

"It's not that. In fact he didn't even sign his name. It was the words that meant the most. That's all."

He looked up at her, "If he didn't sign his name, how do you know that he sent them?"

She laughed, "Who else would send them?"

He shrugged, "I don't know. I was just curious." He looked back at the menu, knowing that he needed the conversation to be dropped. "I'm starving," he said, changing the subject.

She looked in the menu and he casually glanced at her from the corner of his eye. He hoped that the next attempt went more smoothly, because he was bombing out.

***

Tiffany received a call, right after she got out of the shower. She didn't recognize the number, but since she had submitted so many applications she knew she needed to answer it. "Hello?"

"Hello, is this Tiffany Reynolds?"

"Yes, this is she." She said, crossing her fingers.

"Hello, Ms. Reynolds. This is Matthew Riley from Riley advertising. How are you doing?"

She could barely find the words. She couldn't believe the owner was actually calling her. "I...I'm doing great." She replied, trying not to sound too eager.

"Good to hear. I was hoping you could come in today so we could talk. I have received your application and I am very impressed." She could have squealed with pleasure, but she held back.

"That would be great. What time works best for you?"

"How about coming by at eleven o'clock. Do you know where we're located?"

She nodded, realizing that he wouldn't be able to see the gesture. "I do. I will be there. Thank you!"

"You're welcome. See you soon!" The call was disconnected and she stared at the phone. She twirled around her hotel room. She was hoping that this was the break she was looking for. She glanced at the clock, she had two hours to get ready and be there. She knew that it was about thirty minutes away, so she would have plenty of time. She grabbed her classiest outfit she had packed and got dressed. She spent more time on her hair and makeup. She wanted it to be perfect.

She was putting her earrings in, when she heard a knock . She rushed to the door and peeked outside. A guy was standing at her door. She frowned, but then flung the door open. "Hello?"

"Ms. Reynolds?" He asked. She nodded, "Please sign here." He handed her a clipboard. She signed her name and then he handed her a small box. "Have a nice day."

"You too," she replied, absentmindedly. She looked at the package and saw that there was no return address. Her name and the hotel address was handwritten on the front. She recognized the writing, but couldn't immediately place it. She opened up the box and found another box inside. This time it was a velvet box. She opened it up and stared at the necklace. Her eyes got big, finding the gold cross inside. Wrapped around the cross was rubies that alternated with topazes. She pulled it from the box. "It's gorgeous," she spoke, putting it around her neck and going to the mirror. "Perfect to complete the ensemble." She couldn't believe how thoughtful Erick was. His birthday was in

November, representing the topaz birthstone and her birthday was in April, representing the ruby. She ran her hand over the cross.

She had yet to hear back from him when she received the flowers a few days earlier. She picked up the phone and dialed his number again. Again it went straight to his voicemail. "Hey, Erick. I am starting to worry a bit. I haven't heard back from you in a few days. Thank you so much for the necklace. It's gorgeous. Also, the flowers were perfect. I love you." She hung up and glanced one more time in the mirror. She was ready to go land the job.

She called a cab and fifteen minutes she was out the door and heading to Riley Advertising. She was relieved to see that she wasn't nervous. She was anxious though. She paid the cab driver and hurried up the front steps. She was glad that she had brought her portfolio along. She felt professional and ready to make her move.

She approached the desk with confidence. "My name is Tiffany Reynolds. I am here to meet with Matthew Riley."

"Of course, Ms. Reynolds. He will be out in a few minutes. You may have a seat."

She sat down and waited for him to arrive. Like clockwork, it was only a couple of minutes. He walked out with swag, offering his hand to her. "Ms. Reynolds, it is very nice to meet you."

"Likewise," she spoke, standing up. She followed him, past the reception desk.

"Please hold my calls," he stated to the receptionist. They entered a room and he held back for her to go before him. "Please, have a seat."

She took a seat and placed her portfolio down. "I want to thank you for taking the time out to meet with me."

He smiled, "I have made some calls and you have come highly recommended." He stated. "Your previous employer was sorry to see you go."

She blushed, "I had to make a tough decision. I enjoyed working there."

"May I ask why you chose to leave?"

She thought about that, letting out a slow breath. "My fiancé is getting transferred here. So, I had no choice."

He nodded, "It's a good reason." He looked down at her application. "I am very impressed with your resume. I am assuming you have samples of your work."

"Of course," she said, reaching down and opening her briefcase. She took out her campaigns and handed them to him. It was the first step of letting herself out there and she hoped that he liked it.

***

Scott looked up to find Tiffany entering his office. A smile was present on her lips. He stood up. "This is a pleasant surprise." His eyes instantly went to her necklace. He could definitely see that she wore it well.

"I got a job," she said, throwing her arms around him.

He held her close, feeling how much he wanted that to be an everyday occurrence. "That is wonderful news, Tiff." She pulled away and there was so much happiness in her eyes. "I bet Erick is ecstatic."

Her eyes fell to the ground, "He probably would be if I could get ahold of him." She shrugged, "I knew that I would be able to see you."

He tried not to show how much those words meant to him. He pointed to her necklace, "Nice necklace. Is it new?" He wanted to fish to see what she would say. "I see it has rubies and topazes in it."

She smiled, holding the necklace. "Yes, I just got it today. As you know my birthday is in April and Erick's is in November." His face fell. He couldn't believe his luck. Her eyes lit up and she laughed, "I didn't think about that, but so is yours."

He nodded, "The eighteenth. How about him?"

"The twelfth." She replied. She seemed to think about that, "What a coincidence."

"I'll say," He mumbled. "Well, I think that's amazing news about the job. We should celebrate tonight. I can pick you up when I get off work today. It will be about six o'clock. Does that work?"

"That would be great," she smiled. "I'll see you later."

"See you," He called, as she left his office.

He sunk down in his chair and opened up his desk drawer. He pulled the letter out from the corner of his desk. He read through it. It was time to make the next move. He was sure of it. He folded the letter and put it into his jacket pocket. He got up and left his office for another meeting. By the end of the evening she would know exactly how he felt and he could hope that she felt the same.

***

Tiffany tried one more time to call Erick. She groaned in frustration, disconnecting the call. She didn't know why she couldn't get ahold of him. She heard a knock and she went to answer it. "I will be with you in a minute." She called, heading back to get her purse.

"I thought we could have a picnic today. If that's alright with you?"

She frowned, "It's been pretty cold. Are you sure about that?"

He snickered, "Where we're going it won't be cold. I promise."

She thought that was strange, but shrugged. "Whatever. I'm game if you are." She shut her hotel room door and headed with him down the elevator and out the hotel. They got to his car and she saw the picnic basket in the backseat. "It's been awhile since I've been on a picnic," I admitted.

"I think you'll be surprised by the location," he replied. Their eyes connected and he was smiling. She got into the car and he went around to the other side. The drive was quiet, but in a good way. When they turned the corner, she remembered how they had come down this same road a few days ago. She glanced at him and he was just smiling. She didn't bother mentioning it. When they pulled into the driveway, she knew that something was going on.

"What are we doing here?" She asked, staring up at the first house they had visited. A *Sold* sign was in front of it. "What's going on?"

He laughed, "You'll see."

They got out of the car and he grabbed the picnic basket. They then headed up to the front door. She watched as he unlocked the door with a set of keys. "What in the world?" She asked, entering the house.

He turned around, "I bought it."

Her jaw dropped, "Are you serious?"

He laughed, "I knew you would say that. I just fell in love with this house and decided that it was time to make the move. What do you think?"

"I think you are out of your mind." She replied, smacking him on the arm. "This is pretty cool, but sad. You got a house before me and I was the one looking."

He laughed, "I'm sorry, but I didn't want to pass it up."

She had to admit she was a little jealous, but she was also thrilled for him. "Congrats Scott," she leaned up to kiss his cheek, but he turned his head so that her lips were touching his. The kiss lingered for a moment, until she realized what was happening. "Scott..." she said, touching her lips.

"Tiffany, listen to me." He said. He took his hand to her waist and she slowly pulled away.

"I'm getting married," she quickly said, moving backwards.

"He hasn't even called you." He argued.

She glared at him. "He's sent me flowers and a necklace to show me that he is thinking about me. That's all I need."

He moved to her, "Tiffany, I bought you those things." He said.

She opened her mouth, but no words came out. She shook her head, "You're lying. His birthstone..."

"Is my birthstone. You said it yourself. I know your favorite flower. Go with your heart. Do you honestly think I'm making this up?"

She didn't know what to believe. She was going to be Erick's wife and this wasn't supposed to happen like this. "I am getting married," she spoke again.

"To the wrong man," he replied.

"Stop it!" She yelled. "You are my best friend and nothing will ever happen between us."

"Why not? Are you that scared?" He asked, intently staring at her.

"Why are you doing this? I know those gifts came from Erick." She looked away from him, feeling tears stinging the back of her eyes. "Take me home."

"Tiffany, don't....talk to me."

She shook her head, "Take me home." She spoke again. She turned from him and ran from the house. She couldn't let him get to her. She knew the truth and that's what mattered.

***

"Tiffany, won't you please hear me out." Scott said for the hundredth time. "I wouldn't lie to you."

She couldn't stay in that car and listen to him. Nothing seemed real. She reached for her door handle. "Don't call me," she said, with anger in her voice.

Pain was etched on his face. He pulled something from his jacket pocket and placed it in her hand. "Just read it. Please."

She closed her hand on the letter. She anticipated, she would just throw it away, but she didn't say that. "Goodnight," she replied, jumping out of the car and heading into the hotel.

The moment she got inside, she felt the tears fall. She got into the elevator, feeling her body shaking from the tears. When she got out of the elevator, she walked to her room. She opened the door and fell to the bed.

She looked at the folded piece of paper and thought about just throwing it away. Instead, she opened it up and started to read. The more she read the worse she felt. She covered her mouth. The fact that he felt that was shocking to her, but it didn't change the fact that she wasn't available. As she got up, she threw the note into the wastebasket. She heard her cellphone ringing and she grabbed it from her pocket. She sighed with relief, seeing Erick's name across the screen.

"Hello."

"Hey, babe. It's been awhile."

She wanted to argue that that was his fault, but she didn't have the energy. "You have no idea how much I needed to hear your voice." She said, falling back down on the bed.

"I'm sorry I have been out of touch. It's been crazy, but I did get your messages." She held onto his words. It would be a relief to hear him talk about the gifts that he got her. "I must admit, I'm a little confused. What flowers and necklace are you referring to?"

A gasp escaped her lips. This couldn't be. "Um...never mind, I was mistaken." She said, dumbfounded.

"Oh..." he snickered.

She felt a weight in her chest, but tried to get over it. "I got a job today."

There was a long pause, before he spoke again. "You did? There's actually something that I need to tell you."

"I'm listening."

"There has been a change of plans. I was offered a better position if I stay here. It equals more money and more responsibilities. In the long run I can't pass it up."

"You didn't call me. This would be news that you should have told me before I went and got another job."

"I know, baby, but I just found out and I couldn't let you know earlier. It wasn't finalized. Just tell the place that hired you that you're fiancé is staying in New York. They'll understand."

She couldn't find the words to express how upset she was. "I won't understand. This job is giving me opportunities that I don't want to pass up. I love you, but..." her words dropped off.

"What are you trying to say?"

"We barely know each other. You are obviously more wrapped up in your job than I could ever compete with."

"That's not true," he argued.

"Yes...it is." She continued, "It would never work out."

"But..."

"I will mail you the ring back. Good luck and I wish you every bit of happiness."

"Tiffany, don't..." he started, saying the same words that Scott had spoken. She hung up the phone, feeling relief.

She looked at her ring and pulled it off her finger. She placed it on the dresser and went back to the wastebasket. She picked up the letter and reread it. She knew that Scott was someone that could handle a mixture of being with her and working. She grabbed her purse and headed to the door. She needed to talk to him and she hoped there was a cab around.

When she opened the door, she nearly ran right into him. "I, couldn't just leave..." he began, before he could go on she wrapped her hand around his neck and pulled him close to her. Their lips connected and she melted into him. His tongue ran along hers and she pulled from him.

"I'm sorry," she spoke, grabbing his hand and pulling him into the hotel room. "I love you," she spoke, pulling him back to her and wrapping her arms around him. They could talk later. The only thing that mattered to her was showing him how much she cared for him and she would show him that the rest of her life.

******

Second Chances

Brooke felt an immediate attraction to Sean the moment she first saw him at her best friend, Lisa's wedding. Although he was there with a date, Brooke couldn't help but stare at him.

Sean was stunningly handsome, and he had the most dazzling smile she'd ever seen.

When Lisa returned from her honeymoon, she called Brooke and asked her what she thought about Sean.

"I thought he was gorgeous! Too bad he was with a date," Brooke said.

"She's not his girlfriend, and in fact, he seems to be interested in you," Lisa explained.

"You have my permission to give him my phone number," Brooke told Lisa.

"I already did," Lisa replied.

When Sean called her, Brooke was so nervous that she couldn't think of a thing to say. She felt that their conversation was strained at first, but as it progressed, the couple's banter flowed freely and effortlessly.

Brooke learned that Sean was an investment banker who grew up only minutes away from Brooke's hometown.

"I'm sure that we know some of the same people," Sean said.

"Where did you go to high school," Brooke asked.

"Central, how about you?"

"Riverwoods," she replied.

The couple continued on with their small talk for what seemed like an eternity to Brooke, but after a while, Sean finally asked her out.

"What are you doing Saturday night?"

"I don't have plans yet," Brooke said.

Sean asked, "Have you ever been to that new restaurant on Mayfair Street yet?"

"Not yet, but I've been wanting to check it out for the longest time. I've heard that they have the best pub food around and that it has live entertainment on the weekends," Brooke replied.

Brooke didn't want to say anything to Sean, but her ex-boyfriend, Levi was the restaurant's manager.

She and Levi had broken up about a year ago after she found out that he was cheating on her with one of the waitresses he worked with.

Brooke was devastated by the break-up, and was convinced that she would never find love again.

"I'll pick you up at 7," Sean told Brooke.

"Great! I'm looking forward to seeing you."

While Brooke really didn't want to bump into her ex-boyfriend at the restaurant, she kind of hoped that he would see her with Sean.

Levi wasn't the jealous type, but Brooke hoped that if he saw her with another guy, he might regret that he broke up with her.

She recently heard that he and his waitress girlfriend were no longer together, and as far as Brooke knew, he was single.

Levi worked long hours at the restaurant and didn't have a lot of time for a social life.

When Sean arrived to pick her up, Brooke was dazzled by his rugged good looks. He was impeccably dressed and smelled delicious.

"You look absolutely gorgeous," Sean told Brooke.

"Thank you. You don't look so bad, yourself!"

As the couple drove into the restaurant's parking lot, Brooke starting feeling anxious. What would she do if she saw Levi?

She thought about telling Sean that her ex-boyfriend was the manager, but decided against it, at least for now.

The restaurant was dark and cozy, which gave Brooke a sense of comfort. Even if Levi was working, she didn't think that he could possible see her, unless he walked up to her table.

Brooke finally started to relax, knowing that she wouldn't have to encounter an uncomfortable meeting with her ex-boyfriend.

The conversation between she and Sean was flowing nicely until he asked her about her past relationships.

"How long did your last relationship last?"

"About two years," Brooke replied.

"What happened, if you don't mind me asking?"

"Things just didn't work out between us, and we decided to go our separate ways."

Sean continued to press Brooke for answers about her relationship with Levi. Feeling uncomfortable, Brooke finally told him that she didn't want to talk about it anymore. Feeling embarrassed by his boldness, Sean apologized.

After only a couple of hours, Brooke determined that Sean would make a good boyfriend.

She liked the fact that he was considerate of her feelings, had the same job for ten years, was close to his family and had tons of friends.

While Brooke didn't enjoy talking about her past relationships, Sean had no problem doing so.

"My last relationship lasted for about five years, and even though we were in love, we both knew that it wouldn't last."

Sean further explained, "She was quite a bit older than I was and wasn't interested in having a family, which is something that I've always dreamed of."

He also commented that her family wasn't too fond of him because he wasn't established in his career yet.

From the side of her eye, Brooke saw someone resembling like Levi. Her initial reaction was to quickly leave the restaurant, but after thinking about it, she decided to stay.

The person who looked like Levi was stopping at each table conversing with the customers. As it turned out, it was Levi.

Brooke's heart was literally beating out of her chest because Levi, the restaurant manager, was making his way to her and Sean's table.

"Oh my God, here he comes," Brooke said to herself.

Sean sensed that something was wrong, and asked Brooke what it was. At first, she didn't want to volunteer any information about Levi, but she knew that she had to.

"That guy over there, the restaurant manager, is my ex-boyfriend, Levi."

"Do you want to leave?" he asked.

"No, it's okay. I don't care if he sees me."

Before she knew it, Levi was standing at their table and asked, "Hi guys, is everything alright?

At first, Levi didn't notice that it was Brooke sitting at the table because he was looking at Levi when he greeted them.

As soon as he discovered it was her, he exclaimed, "Brooke, it's good to see you again!"

"Nice to see you too, Levi."

Brooke introduced Levi to Sean, and she could tell that they both felt uncomfortable when the shook hands.

Sean as was classy as ever during the introduction and he even engaged Levi in a conversation about the restaurant.

"This is such a great place. How long have you been working here?"

Levi answered, "I really enjoy it here. I've been with the restaurant for about three years."

He further added, "management is great and my co-workers are cool."

For some reason, Brooke was starting to get annoyed at how well the two guys were getting along.

After a few more minutes of small talk, Levi excused himself so that he could get back to work.

Before he left the table, however, he slipped a note into Brooke's purse, which was hanging off the back of her chair.

She didn't discover the note until the next morning, when she was looking for some gum.

The note read: "Brooke, you took my breath away when I saw you tonight. After seeing you, I realized that I made a terrible mistake in letting you go.

I know that you've moved on with your life, and I'm really happy for you, but sad at the same time."

Levi went on to say, "I am so sorry for hurting you and for turning your life upside down. If you could find it in your heart to forgive me, I'd be forever grateful.

Please, Brooke, I'm begging for another chance. I've been constantly thinking about you for months, and I can't get you out of my mind. Please call me. I love you, Brooke."

Brooke was stunned. Even in her wildest dream, she would have never guessed that Levi was still in love with her.

In fact, she assumed that she was simply a distant memory in his mind.

While she was flattered to learn that he still had strong feelings for her, she had no desire to reconnect with him.

Brooke finally told Sean about what happened between her and Levi and how he cheated on her with one of the waitresses he works with.

Sean seemed to sympathize with Levi and even went so far as to say, "well you guys weren't engaged or anything, so I really don't see a problem with it."

While it was true that Brooke and Levi weren't engaged, they had a mutually exclusive relationship with an understanding that neither one of them would see other people.

After Sean's snarky comment, Brooke's entire impression of him changed for the worst.

This wasn't the only uncaring comment he made either. He also mentioned that he really didn't blame Levi for cheating on her because the temptation of being surrounded by so many beautiful cocktail waitresses would make any man stray.

Brooke couldn't believe what she was hearing, and she vowed that if Sean made one more snotty remark, she was going to stop seeing him.

In fact, the better Brooke got to know him, the more appealing Levi became.

While Levi did cheat on her, he always treated with her with the utmost respect and kindness throughout the duration of their relationship. She even feels partially to blame for their break up.

Brooke always pressured Levi into getting a better paying job and furthering his education.

She also demanded all of his time. Levi worked long hours, and he sometimes didn't get home until after midnight.

Brooke didn't care. She would often demand that he come over after work, even if it was late. Levi always complied, and never gave her a hard time about it.

This doesn't justify his cheating, but Brooke was now starting to realize that she may have driven him right into the arms of another women.

One who was understanding, patient and not so demanding.

In fact, one of Brooke's co-workers told her that Levi's relationship with the cocktail waitress was really staring to heat up.

Brooke found this disturbing, especially since he recently professed his love for her through his letter.

Sean's behavior toward Brooke was starting to turn her off more and more. He always wanted to talk about her relationship with Levi, and even started pressuring her into revealing the most intimate details of their sex life.

Sean often asked, "Did you enjoy having sex with him?"

He further inquired, "Who was better in bed, Levi or me?"

Brooke replied, "You're being so intrusive and I resent all the questions." She also told him, "I'm starting to think that we should take a break from each other.

We used to be so happy and always had fun together. Now, there's always conflict."

"The reason there's so much conflict is because you don't want to share anything with me.

When I ask you for details about your relationship with Levi, I expect you to be forthcoming. You're so secretive about everything. I don't understand it," Sean remarked.

Brooke's responded, "I'm hesitant to talk about my former relationships because it's really none of your business. I don't ask you about the intimate details of your past relationships."

Sean was starting to fall in love with Brooke, but he didn't know how to tell her.

After all, they've only been dating for a short time, and he didn't want to come on too strong.

He knew that his prying would be a turn-off, but for some reason, he couldn't help it.

He didn't want to lose Brooke by being too possessive because he considered her his "dream girl."

The couple eventually decided to take a break from one another, and stopped dating for about a month.

During this time, Brooke re-evaluated her feelings for Levi. His note made her feel special, and deep down, she knew that he loved her.

The question was, however, did she still love him?

While she often thought about Levi, Brooke was staring to miss Sean.

She wondered if he felt the same way, so one night, after having a few drinks with some friends, she decided to call him.

"Remember me?" she coyly asked.

"I thought I'd never hear from you again," Sean answered.

"I really miss you, and came to realize just how much I care for you," Brooke said. "Can we meet for dinner next week to talk."

"Next week isn't good for me because I'm going to New York to visit my parents," Sean answered.

Brooke's heart sank. She was now convinced that Sean was no longer interested in her.

"How about Friday of next week?" he asked.

Excited, Brooke responded, "That sounds great, Sean. I can't wait to see you."

Brooke was anticipating her date with Sean and she hoped that they would be able to patch things up between them.

Even though he started acting like a jerk at the end, Brooke knew that he had a good heart, and that he genuinely cared about her.

When Sean picked her up, Brooke could barely catch her breath. He looked amazingly handsome and sexy.

They hugged for what seemed like an eternity, and being with him felt natural and right to Brooke.

The restaurant was romantic and the talk was sweet. By the time they got back to Brooke's house, they could hardly keep their hands off one another.

"Would you like to come in for a cup of coffee?" Brooke asked.

"I would love to."

They sat on the couch and starting kissing. Sean gently put his hands on Brooke's blouse. "I know I said I wanted to take things slow, but I'm not so sure now, so just go for it," she said.

He quickly ripped the blouse from her toned body and it fell to the floor.

His eager lips kissed her neck, while her hands unbuttoned his shirt, removing it from the waistband of his pants.

Brooke started out slowly, but then decided to bust open his shirt in the same manner in which Sean busted opened her blouse.

Her quivering hands found their way down his muscular chest, while he hungrily continued to kiss her.

Brooke arched her back, moaning each time he kissed her.

His strong hands rubbed her back, as he slowly took off her bra. Her ample breasts pressed firmly against his waiting chest.

Her hands unzipped his pants and she quickly removed them. Sean's hands went to his underwear while Brooke tugged on them to get them off.

He kissed her breasts while she eyed his ample erection. She was getting more and more excited with every glance, and when he undid the zipper on her dress, she was consumed with desire.

His hands went to her panties, looping his slender fingers through them, gently pulling them off her body.

Before Brooke had time to anticipate Sean's next move, she felt him pick her up, laying her down on the bed.

Their lips finally met, his eager tongue darting inside her mouth. As their tongues intertwined, his hands massaged her ample breasts, savoring the softness of her supple skin.

As Sean was ready to make love to Brooke, he hesitated. "Damn it, I don't have a condom," pulling back in disappointment.

She pulled him even closer. "Don't worry, I'm on the pill," she soothed, as they kissed and he penetrated her.

"It feels so good" she softly said, arching her back, but never breaking away from his kiss. His thrusts are deliberate and intense, which forces her to lose contact with his lips. It felt like a dream.

While one of Brooke's arms was holding onto Sean, she tried to grasp onto anything she could to hold onto as her body bucked up against his, finally choosing the side of the nightstand.

He had a hunger that she never experienced before. "Damn...yes...yes" he groaned, holding her even tighter to his body.

She could feel him pulsating within her, "God, yes..." she cried. She sighed deeply, almost unable to move, while his rhythmic grinding came to a halt. "That was amazing," she whispered.

As Brooke was basking in the afterglow, she felt Sean's hands moving up her legs, gingerly caressing her.

She wasn't sure what he was going to do, but when she felt his finger gently penetrate her, she moaned, savoring his every move.

In addition to using his finger, he began using his tongue to tease her.

As his tongue glided in and out of her, she reached down and grabbed his head to pull him in even closer to her.

After the interlude was over, Brooke was surprised at her lack of emotion towards Sean.

In fact, during the entire lovemaking session, she was thinking about Levi. She knew that it wasn't fair to Sean, but she couldn't help how she felt.

Had Levi never left that note in her purse, she feels she would have been better off. All these months, she barely thought of Levi. She was moving on with her life and socializing more than ever.

"Sean, I enjoyed our time together, but I can't help but feel that we're not right for each other."

"What about last night," he questioned.

"Last night was great, but there was something missing," Brooke replied.

She further explained, "I don't know how to explain it. I feel as though I should have been into it more, but I wasn't."

"Were you thinking about that jerk, Levi while we were making love?" he asked.

"Sean, I don't want to lie to you. Ever since I saw Levi at the restaurant, I can't get him out of my mind. He and I shared years together, and it's hard to forget about him. I thought I was starting to get him out of my mind once and for all, but seeing him again sparked some old feelings inside me."

"Brooke, please give me a chance to make you happy. I know I can make you forget all about Levi. You're just confused because you saw him again after all those months. The feelings you have for him aren't love. You're just confused."

"Maybe you're right, Sean," Brooke said. She further remarked, "Thank you for being so patient with me. I guess I am confused."

Brooke ended up giving Sean another chance, but as the weeks went by, she still couldn't stop thinking about Levi. She knew that she wanted to call him to talk about a reconciliation.

As she dialed his number, Brooke was shaking. She was hoping that his voicemail would pick up so that she could leave a message. It didn't.

"Hello?"

"Hi Levi, it's Brooke."

Levi's voice cracked as though he were starting to cry.

"Hi baby, I miss you so much. We should still be together. I really screwed things up between us."

"What have you been up to, and how serious are you with that guy I saw you with at the restaurant?"

"We've been dating for a while, and while we're semi-serious, our relationship can't compare with the one we had," Brooke said.

"Does this mean that I have a chance?" Levi asked.

"A very good chance," she said.

Brooke and Levi decided to meet at a neighborhood coffee shop, and when they first saw each other, they hugged and cried.

They both commented on how being together felt so right, and that neither one of them had found true happiness since the break up.

The couple decided that they wanted to spend the rest of their lives together, but they would first have to break the news to their current partners.

Brooke knew that Sean would take it hard, but he was a strong enough person that he would bounce back quickly and get on with his life.

Levi's current girlfriend, on the other hand, might not take it so well. She had been pressuring him for an engagement ring because she wanted to settle down and have a family with him.

"Let's go away for the weekend," Levi suggested.

While Brooke normally would have jumped at the chance to have Levi all to herself for an entire weekend, she didn't feel right about it. She wanted to end things with Sean before taking Levi up on his offer.

It disturbed her that Levi would suggest going away together before ending it with his current girlfriend.

"You'll have to end your relationship before I'll go away with you."

Levi reasoned, "I'll have a talk with her when I get back."

It was right then and there that Brooke decided she didn't want anything more to do with Levi.

He planned on cheating on his girlfriend just like he cheated on her. This brought back so many negative memories, and she really sympathized with the other woman.

"I see that you haven't changed much. You don't have a moral compass," Brooke said.

"Come on, Brooke, give me a break. I've been under a lot of stress lately. The restaurant is crazy busy, and I've been working 80 hours a week."

Levi further explained, "All I ask is that you give me another week to end the relationship. You'll see, Brooke. I'll do right by you."

"I'm sorry Levi. This isn't going to work out." I can't be with someone who seems like a serial cheater. You cheated on me, and now you're scheming to cheat on her."

"Brooke, you don't understand," Levi argued.

"Unfortunately, Levi, I do."

"I'd never be able to trust you. How do you expect me to love you when I can't trust you?"

"Goodbye, Levi."

Surprisingly, Brooke wasn't too upset about how it all played out. She felt worse thinking about how she hurt Sean when she broke up with him.

She even wondered if Sean would take her back. She hated the dating scene, and always preferred to be in a relationship, even if it did have some ups and downs.

Brooke was looking forward to reconnecting with Sean. She had a feeling that he was thinking about her, and would welcome her back with open arms.

They were always so connected to each other, and they both assumed that they would end up getting married one day.

Brooke couldn't decide on whether to text Sean or to call him. She longed to hear his voice, and hoped he would feel the same.

She dialed his cell, but he didn't answer. She didn't leave a message, but instead, decided to call him on the home phone.

After the phone rang about three times, someone answered it.

"Hello?"

Brooke was confused, because the person who answered the phone was a woman. She must have dialed the wrong number.

"I'm sorry, I think I have the wrong number," Brooke said.

"Who were you trying to reach?" the woman asked.

"A friend of mine named Sean," Brooke replied.

"You have the right number. This is his wife. Who can I say is calling?"

"Never mind. I'm sorry to have bothered you."

Badly shaken, Brooke trembled as she disconnected the call. How could Sean have met someone and gotten himself married in such a short period of time?

She felt that her dreams were shattered. She lost two men that she loved to other women. Maybe it was time for a change of pace, she thought.

Brooke decided to pack up and move to Florida, where she had family. She took a job in retail until she could find something in her field. While her new life wasn't exciting by any stretch of the imagination, it was quiet and serene.

If she met someone, it would be great. If not, she wasn't going to stress out about it. As the week turned into months, Brooke started feeling depressed.

Her social life was almost non-existent, and her job bored her to tears. While she had family in Florida, they were much older than she was, and they lived hundreds of miles away.

On a whim, Brooke decided to enroll in a cooking class at the local park district. She always loved to cook, but never considered herself a gourmet. Not only would the class give her the opportunity to brush up on her culinary skills, but she also might meet some new friends.

Brooke had so much fun on the first night of the class. The people were outgoing and welcoming, and the group was very diverse. Although Brooke was happy to meet the women the class, she was more intrigued by the tall, handsome stockbroker who also signed up to learn how to cook.

"Hi, I'm Jack. What's your name?"

"Brooke. It's nice to meet you, Jack."

She couldn't believe her luck. Not only was she engaged in an activity that she enjoyed, but she also met a guy. While she never met Jack before, he looked so familiar. In fact, he looked a lot like Levi, much to her dismay.

During the fourth cooking class, Jack asked Brooke out for coffee. She eagerly said "yes," but was shocked to discover who he was.

"Have you always lived in Florida," Brooke asked.

"No, I actually just moved here to manage a restaurant. My brother, with whom I'm estranged from, used to manage it, but ran it into the ground. The restaurant is owned by our grandparents, and when they discovered that he had been fooling around with all the waitresses and stealing money from the business, they fired him and sort of disowned him."

Jack further explained, "My brother has since moved out of state, and from what I hear, he's managing another restaurant."

A chill ran down Brooke's spine. Right then and there, she knew that Jack was Levi's brother.

"What's your brother's name?"

"Levi," Jack replied.

Brooke didn't let on that she was in a relationship with Levi. If things between them were to get serious, she would tell him. But for now, she didn't see a reason to.

Both Brooke and Jack enjoyed each other's company so much that they decided to go out on a real date. One date led to another, and before she knew it, the couple was engaged.

Through the grapevine, both Sean and Levi got wind of Brooke's upcoming wedding. By this time, Sean was already divorced from his wife, and Levi had broken up with his girlfriend. They each sent Brooke congratulatory emails, professed their love for her and revealed that she was truly "the one who got away."

******

About the Author

J.L. Ryan is a bestselling author who has written over 50 books, including the wildly popular Billionaire Boys Club, Billionaire Games, Billionaire Bachelors, and Adventures In Romance. Ryan has also attended numerous book signings and writer's conventions including Romance Writers Of America Conferences. Living in New York, J.L. enjoys spending time with family and friends, volunteering at a large metropolitan homeless shelter, and working in the dog rescue community.

www.ingramcontent.com/pod-product-compliance
Lightning Source LLC
Chambersburg PA
CBHW021959190626
46808CB00017B/2838